Tales of the Forbidden

Also by Georg Engel from K A Nitz:

Thy Neighbour's Wife

The Famine Village and Other Tales

Sorceress Circe: A Berlin Romance

The Burden

The Fear Before the Wife

Tales of the Forbidden

Georg Engel

K A Nitz
WELLINGTON

Contents

THE FORBIDDEN INTOXICATION

The Forbidden Intoxication

It was still dark in the little cottage. The dawn was contending with the night. Pale shadows ran over the walls like little grey mice coming from nothing and vanishing into nothing.

Then Martin Kriews, the eternally unemployed, turned for the first time on his red and white checkered sack of straw. A comfortable, awakening grunting could be heard. Then he gently, peacefully struck with his fist at the neighbouring sack of straw.

"Sweety," he yawned, "it's such a beautiful day again. The sun shines. Have a look, quite red" — at the same time, he stared into the weaving black shadows, and had the awareness that the sun was stepping closer and closer to him, with a coppery red face, exactly like the wife of the innkeeper Krey, that loving womanhood who had just the evening before poured him a small pail of the just newly distilled cheery and peppermint liqueur with affectionate verve into his huge hip flask.

And what was most enviable, she had forgotten about the payment entirely again in the surge of business.

"Sweety," Martin Kriews said serenely to the motionless sack of straw. "She surely loves me, Krey's dear wife. They all love me. Absolutely, Sophie, the people of the world are all kindhearted. I tell you, Sophie, they are all kindhearted. Yesterday, for example, I was walking past the window of the County Commissioner, von Pitak. There he was standing, and making himself a quite bitterly angry face because a bottle of red wine which he had just wanted to drink for breakfast had gone off. Well, what was great about that now? It could have been a bit worse. Nothing more. And what does the highborn noble man do now? He simply offers it to me out the window, and says, 'Kriews, I want to give you something.' — Now look, Sophie, such noble-mindedness."

Silence.

The little grey mice were running serenely over the walls, and the second sack of straw remained in silence.

Then Martin Kriews turned around again comforted, bit a corner of his bed cover, and murmured to himself, "If I just knew who had shoved the fine roast hare into my mouth? Did my Sophie do that? Or Mrs Krey? Or the highborn County Commissioner, von Pitak, who is so noble-minded? The devil knows, people are such dear creatures."

And with that, he began to lapse again into a strangely melodious twang.

***

At six o'clock in the morning, the bleak November day had lifted far enough that the little grey mice no longer felt safe on the walls, but fled in all directions. Straight to the head of Martin Kriews where an enormous cobweb swayed over the covers, they whizzed right there with a gentle chirp. At this moment, the smashed window casement was rattling imperceptibly, scantily patched up with straw, rags, and cardboard. But that happened only because Wilhelm Pölk, the fiance of Kriew's only daughter, Helene, was taking his leave, or had just arrived.

The dreamily rapt father could not work that out exactly, it was just one of those things which could not be established so easily.

Then Martin Kriews straightened up for the second time. "What a joy, Sophie," he rose breathing deeply, "when two are so fond of each other. That is for a set of parents the happiest and most sublime thing of all. Wife, just look at Wilhelm's red face. I tell you, it's not beaming from the cold or chilblains, it's glowing with love. Wife, my sweety, didn't I also stand before your window once like that? But the truth, the glory. Next to you, our daughter is a pure, white tallow candle. God, sweety, what a high noble beauty you were. Not all your womandhood was so pretty and plump. And if others had also hatched with your heat pimples — no, no, Sophie, I just mean — you see, for the pimples were something fantastical for me, something not everyone had. For people must have something special. And since then, wife, you have become even more beautiful." It could have occurred to the gentle Kriews, the eternally unemployed, to some extent that only a very suspect clearing of her throat ever answered all these homages. In fact, Mrs Sophie Kriews, who was still being extolled by Martin, like the blind singer of the Iliad had paid homage to the Queen of Sparta in ancient times, had meanwhile peeled herself out of the neighbouring sack of straw. And see, you must confess with a look at the so highly praised woman that Kriews, the husband, possesses an unusually contented and selfless nature. For Sophie, the day labourer's wife, who with the constant handicap of her husband carried out for him all external matters like harvesting potatoes, gathering straw, hauling wood, and yardwork; Sophie had actually far too much of the "special" in her. The 'o' shaped configuration of her feet, well yes, that arose from the constant stooping when gathering potatoes. That was thus to be excused. But why she was adorned with a growth on her left shoulder, that only dear God had to answer for with her creation, and it could be seen by Martin after all as a little piquant irregularity. What meanwhile set the most decisive monument to his lack of prejudice was the state of Sophie's complexion. For it had to be admitted unfortunately that she hosted countless boils and chilblains on her cheeks which had, as a result of this invasion, assumed the revolutionary colours of France, namely blue, white, and red. And truly, to ignore this required the monstrously happy idealism of Martin Kriews, the eternally unemployed.

They were sitting by the tottery birch table and drinking what Sophie, again with her suspect clearing of the throat, had called 'coffee'. Martin, scantily clad in woolen undergarments, Sophie fully armoured for daily work, a pickaxe in her hand.

There the following parting conversation unwound between husband and wife.

"Sophie, are you going now?"

"Yes, Kriews," a sharp voice returned.

"Wife, what an industrious woman you are. Haven't I had a great bit of fortune with you. How you keep everything in order, and how clean it doesn't look with us — —", here he kicked about with his loose sock in a heap of rubbish which had indeed gathered under the table, but which made the smoothness and comfort of the floor almost like a thick Smyrna carpet. "Yes, what I wanted to say, you are something royal, wife. See, you're now going into the yard to work, and I'll stay back here for a bit longer, and build up my strength. There is still a little bottle of juniper there. And when I have then built up my strength, then I will go into town, and look for work again. But I'll be home again for lunch, wife. For if I don't see your dear face, then I won't like the taste. And in the afternoon, wife, I'll go looking for work again. See, that way I'll make good use of my day."

"Yes," the woman said, already in the doorway, and her red and blue cheeks began glowing like fireworks. "This time, Kriews, I will also make good use of my day. You will be surprised."

"No, wife."

"Why not?"

"Wife, because only the absolute best and loveliest can come from you. For you, Sophie, are a holy angel."

"So?" the woman whispered, and the word sounded as if a vinegar pot were being emptied, "well, then take care, my treasure. Adieu, Kriews."

"Farewell, my darling."

The door creaked back into its lock, and hardly had the steps of the departing woman died away, than Martin, the eternally unemployed, rose, crept under the stove bench, and fetched out a bottle wrapped thickly in cloth.

"You must tend to it," he said in an indoctrinating way. "Juniper is a vulnerable sort. It can easily summon a cold." With that he sat down at the table, and in a sudden outburst of blissfulness, he growled to himself:

> Man's highest happiness on earth
> Is to loved and be loved.

***

"Come in," the County Commissioner von Pitak demanded, and after the Police Constable had entered in his green uniform with the white bandolier and the clinking sabre, he rose a little from the comfortable chaise longue, polished his monocle, and asked very affectionately, "Well, dear Böttcher, which gruesome street ballad are you bringing back?"

The Constable rattled his spurs a little before he pointed behind himself to disapprovingly state, "At your command, Commissioner, we can't get rid of the woman."

"Well, what does she want then? The day for pauper relief applications is Friday."

"At your command, Commissioner, that is not it. The woman wants something quite odd."

"Well, thunderbolts, what does she want then? Does she desire the succession to the throne in Prussia? It isn't consultation hour today."

"At your command, Commissioner, that we have also indicated to her. But then she brought the Pastor along with her."

"What?" the County Commissioner was reminded, as he quickly rose, to brush the crease his trousers right and set the monocle business-like before his sharp, light blue eye. "Pastor Schöning? Yes, man, for God's sake, what's with you then? How can you let the venerable gentleman even wait for a minute? It's like there's no sense to be had in the office. Well, then. I allow the re-quest obviously. Thunderbolts, has a chair hopefully been offered to the Pastor?"

"At your command, Commissioner. The Pastor is seated. The woman stands."

"Well, good. So let them enter immediately."

At that the heels are struck together, the sabre and spurs rattle, the broad, green uniformed figure van-ishes, and after a few moments, you can hear from the adjoining reception room soft, shuffling steps approach-ing and in-between the clatter of rough clogs.

"These wenches are born troublemakers," the County Commissioner murmurs, then sunshine draws across his countenance while he receives the dignified, white haired clergyman with a deep, gentlemanly bow.

"Oh, please — please, Pastor, take the best place — no idea that you were waiting some time — but in these petty officials, no trace of manners is to be found — will change with time of course — see work in that — no, please, there on the sofa. — And you, dear woman, set aside the clogs perhaps for the time being please — it's only because of my carpet. Now then, Pastor, at your service."

From the sofa, a quite soft, discreet cough sounds, while the clergyman gently rocks his fine, smooth-shaven, old man's countenance. Then he strokes his black glacé gloves with pleasure, sedately entwines his fingers, and begins with a gentle, practised theologian's voice, "Yes, my most admirable gentleman, von Pitak, to see salvation in the distance, perhaps in earthly sanctions, I believe that, through the powers of compulsion which are placed in your hand, you will not only deliver a material service to Mrs Kriews here, but even be able to lead a lost, foundering human life back into the light of day again."

The County Commissioner scrapes a little in his chair, skims with a sideglance behind his monocle the wizened figure of the day labourer's wife, and endeavours with a gentle bow to respond that he would of course be ready with pleasure for such moral aid. 'Thunderbolts, what might be wrong with this woman?' flies at the same time lightning quick through his thoughts. But he adds aloud, "Quite right, Pastor — of course, very delighted to be chosen for such cooperation — but may I perhaps request something clearer —"

"Certainly, my admirable friend, the matter is not entirely easy for me. You know, a power of compulsion does not accompany my office well. Nevertheless though, you understand, nevertheless I hold myself authorised to request of you —"

"Yes," the woman throws in-between from the background.

"Now, the matter doesn't, admittedly, tolerate any postponement," Pastor Schöning continues, while he points with his finely gloved hand expressively at Mrs Kriews. "You see, my dear friend, after thorough consideration and real inward determination, I would like to ask you, shall we say, informally request, that the husband of this poor woman who is known to me to be absolutely hardworking and God-fearing — hm, yes, it is difficult to express such a thing — so I would like to arrange for the day labourer Martin Kriews of Lower Pümplow to be placed on the register of drunkards."

"Ah, indeed," the County Commissioner repeats, whereby he begins polishing his monocle with his handkerchief, as if this demand does not quite come at a good time for him, "of course, Pastor, your information suffices completely for me. On the other hand, however, I must not refrain from indicating to you that higher places — yes, as said, you don't like to see this list becoming to covered with names. Have you, Pastor — I ask forgiveness for the question — already convinced yourself of the constant, not to be ameliorated drunkenness of the aforementioned Kriews?"

Here, however, the clergyman rocks his head gently like a leaf quivering in the cold wind, and gentle disapproval rings out from his soft voice.

"Would I be sitting here otherwise, Mr von Pitak? And believe me, yes, do you in all seriousness consider it possible that a wife, who has provided for the household with obedience and respect up to now, gifted her husband a daughter, and lived with him in the stipulated Christian coexistence up to this day, yes, do you not believe yourself that such a wife only forsakes the secrets of her family with bleeding heart and the greatest torment of her soul?"

"Certainly, Pastor — obviously my view entirely — but — unpleasant story."

The County Commissioner rises, sticks his hands in his sidepockets, and plants himself before the day labourer's wife.

"Well, tell me, please, dear woman, does he get drunk every day now?"

"The night too, Commissioner."

"What, the night too? Here, in fact, a quite unusual case appears to exist. Now tell me please, you want thus to indicate by your information that the alcoholic needs of your husband are placing the basis of your marriage in question, even to an extent being destroyed? That is actually the government's regulatory requirement."

Mrs Kriews bangs defiantly with her pick on the floor so that the County Commissioner quivers nervously, "Yes, he's destroying everything."

"Well good. And you are now of the view that a public prohibition on dispensing to your husband spirits in any form may contribute vitally to his improvement? Is that right?"

"That unfortunately may hardly be doubted surely," Pastor Schöning slides in here. "If ever in the life of the state, change and remedy is to be made by a hard, seemingly arbitrary measure, then our action is warranted just now in this case. Take courage, dear woman, with God's gracious help, and through the care of the Commissioner, the long absent husband will be returned to you, the caring father to the house, and a joyfully working citizen to the state. Commissioner von Pitak, I thank you, also in the name of this poor, tormented woman, for your sympathetic willingness. Admittedly, I did not expect any different."

The Pastor rises, stretches both hands out to the Commissioner, and although the latter seems for a moment to be not quite in agreement over his own willingness, the gentle authority of the clergyman has its affect.

"Wonderful, Pastor, as said, these cases are not well looked on by and large, but since the facts of the case were so completely clear, I believe I owe you the broadest good-will on this special point. Please, a moment."

With that he opens the white lacquered door which leads into the adjoining reception.

"Constable Böttcher."

"At your command, Commissioner."

"Get straight on your hack. In the County Gazette, the decree is to be printed that spirits in any form may not be supplied to the day labourer Martin Kriews of Lower Pümplow by any tavern or distillery, or a bar or shop within our county on pain of a fine of one hundred marks. This decree is to be delivered by you immediately in person to the mayor of Lower Pümplow."

And turning backwards, von Pitak added ingratiatingly to his visitors, "You are pleased with me, Pastor? Do you wish for anything else, dear woman?"

"No, Commissioner. Now it's alright. Now rejoice, Kriews."

But the Pastor suggests, in saying goodbye, "By human estimation, we have today fostered an agreeable work."

***

It should have made for a cheerful afternoon's coffee.

"But I am curious now," Mrs Sophie Kriews said to her daughter as well as her prospective son-in-law, with whom she was sitting around the tottery birch table, while the illumination of the room originated from a dripping tallow candle which had been placed on the low brick hearth.

"Yes, mother," the bridegroom-to-be agreed, as he greedily looked at a slice of bread which his dear prospective mother-in-law was just beginning to coat with plum jam. "Watch, the business will be quite funny."

But the expectations of people are deluded, something else always steps out from the future's clouded gates.

"Yikes," Mrs Kriews suddenly cried.

"Yikes," her daughter and future son-in-law agreed.

And God, what a strange figure appeared just then in the twisted doorway. No, no, that could never have been Martin Kriews, the smiling man, the eternally meek-natured man. It was a sombre, torn up conception of a man who ducked and looked around with timid, peering glances into the small room.

Then the strange creature crept closer to those waiting. He hewed his fist dully against the table so that the mugs rattled together, and the slice of bread with plum jam which Sophie was just then wanting to guide to her mouth turned unexpectedly with its coated side onto the table.

"Yikes," cried Sophie appalled.

"Yikes," the prospective son-in-law followed this time too, although his sympathy lay more with the coveted slice of bread.

"Kriews, what's with you?" his wife inquired, forgetting to close her mouth out of shock.

Only the man questioned did not seem to be in the mood for conducting a popular conversation. On the contrary, he thumped wildly with his fist on the table until he finally emitted, whispering hoarsely like a vicious animal, "Why are you sitting here? What use is company here? What does Wilhelm Pölk want here? Who exactly is Wilhelm Pölk? I don't know him. Don't know his intentions. Does he have intentions exactly? As a father, I ask does he have intentions?"

"But husband," Sophie objected, on the whole not understanding, while she attempted to push the somewhat upset slice of bread into the hand of her prospective son-in-law to appease him. "Husband, what's the matter with you?"

"What's the matter? Lots is the matter with me. But whom does that concern? Am I not master in my own house? Wife, I just asked, am I master? Or am I not master? Thunder and lightning, now open your mouth."

Only the good wife could not yield a single word from shock, and this upset her so-suddenly-bettered husband still more.

"Look at how it is here?" he cried with renewed seething, and kicked at the same time against the tottery table so that it let out a painful groan.

"Doesn't it look here like Sodom and Gomorrah?", here he stooped, reached under the table, and brought forth a blunted broom which Sophie had laid down there trustfully in her efforts at cleanliness.

"Well? You women?" the offended master of the house raged, "and that should be cleanliness? Am I in a cow's stall? Am I in a pigsty? Where am I actually? I just want to know, please, where am I?"

"Yes, but, dear father," the prospective bridegroom wanted to object here, but just the voice of this innocent quickened the irritated father to the peak of his fury.

"Look, it wants to speak with me here. In my own paternal home, it speaks with me. Tell me, are you not ashamed at all in your morals? Would you like to look at the doors a bit from the outside for once? Out!" he roared, suddenly intensifying, "out. It is unfitting to me, out, I say, out of my paternal house."

And with that, the foaming man grasped the arm of the dumbfounded suitor, and shoved him together with his wailing fiance roughly out the door of the cottage.

"Father," the daughter begged from outside, "father, for God's sake ..."

"Oh well, I am fathered out, I must bring some order to my clean home. I'm obliged to do it as a noble patriarch of the family. And absolutely, now get a grip, you bratty package. For now I want to have a neat discussion with the woman present here.

So Mrs Sophie Kriews now learnt the consequences of her reforming deed.

Everywhere in Lower Pümplow, the Commissioner's edict had already become known. Even the lovely Mrs Krey had ached for the pitiable Martin, but had nevertheless had him ordered from her tavern by a servant.

Then he had run to the shopkeeper.

Nothing. Forbidden.

He had raced into the town. God, a thunderstorm. Even here it had already become known by public notice. Was there then no justice anymore? He wanted to pay with those groschen which he had begged for on the country road by honest endeavours. And in spite of everything, no? Hound, damned hound. How did the world have the right to meddle in his most sacred, most personal affairs?

"Woman!" Kriews shouted, cherry brown with fury. "Do I worry about the people? What have they to worry about me here? Soon they will probably come and count the boils and chilblains in your face. Thunderbolts, woman," he broke off suddenly, and stared at his other half in measureless astonishment, "why on earth do you look like that? Don't you look a bit as if lightning has struck your upper body? And its green and blue lighting would now still be left behind? Disgusting, who would have thought it? Sophie, you're ugly as an old monkey. Have you just misplaced yourself in all the years? Or are you only since this afternoon such an old plague? Ugh! When someone looks at you, wife, they'd want to wear glasses made of shoe soles so that they can't see through them. No, and the entire premises here as well. I won't put up with this dirtiness any longer. Now order will prevail."

With these words, good Kriews grasped the broom stub, worked it as though possessed into the corners, and stood at once enveloped in a grey cloud of dust which deprived him of the sight of his appalled wife. But she would anyhow not remain a minute longer alone with the blustering man. Half numbed, she fled out of her usually so peaceful cottage, which had been the site of gently whispered words of love for twenty long years, and wandered out to the dark country road, sobbing softly to herself.

Thus she walked along the sodden country path while the November rain streamed down smooth and unrelenting.

Something barked at her through the night. She started. Would that perhaps be the dog of the shepherd Sturm? Certainly, certainly! About this time, the old man usually came along the village street to carry out the feeding of his flock of sheep in the stalls. And shepherd Sturm, wasn't he the wise man of the village? Couldn't he heal manias and tell the future? Yes, yes, shepherd Sturm was certainly also the man to explain the miracle which had occurred in her house just at this moment.

"Ye — ye — ye —" she suddenly wailed loudly to herself.

The shepherd stopped. "What's the matter with you, my daughter?" the tall thin man asked, while Karo, his dog, sprang around the pair barking loudly.

Then Mrs Kriews bewailed her hardship with trembling to the listener. The shepherd thought for a long time. Then he rubbed his nose vigorously, pulled his cap over his forehead, and whistled to himself a few times, as he tended always to observe when he wanted to order a row of philosophial thoughts. After that he finally began, "Now I know everything, my daughter. The matter is one of the reversed illnesses where the cure is worse than the malady. But the professors in the town don't understand anything about it, and right now, you don't understand anything about it. But look, with God's gracious help, a remedy for it grows, and that I will show you now. Come with me."

Half an hour later, the little cottage was booming with the delighted laughter of Martin Kriews, the eternally unemployed, again, for see, between him and his visitor, the old shepherd Sturm, paraded a giant bottle of the most beautiful black cherry liqueur which the shepherd had conjured up, and strengthened with a special powder.

Yes, whoever just took a glass of this lovely drink travelled directly like the prophet Elias in a fiery chariot to heaven. And before the chariot of Martin, the blissful smiler, seven such radiantly red cloud-horses were already harnessed. It flew just so, clip-clopped, and swished.

"Wife," the eternally happy man cried, "wife, I don't know anything at all, I probably slept badly in the afternoon, and dreamt something quite curious. Just think, my sweety, it seemed to me as if I had swept up here. Now just think, such a stupidity with your cleanliness, when it looks so sparkling and shiny that the German Emperor could eat with the Russian Emperor off our floor. And then, wife, I think, then I even tossed Wilhelm Pölk out of here in my dream. Now take Wilhelm Pölk, the sprucest and smartest man, with a disposition like a nobleman. No, how could anyone, my sweety." And breaking off, he suddenly slung his arm around Sophie's neck, and stammered in rapt delight, "Don't take offense, shepherd Sturm, I know well that it is not fitting for a good patriarch, but what has my Sophie not got for a white swan's neck. Doesn't she look like Snow White come alive in the glass coffin with the seven dwarves? No, Sophie, our daughter Helene is certainly beautiful and virtuous. But next to you, wife, I can simply feel sorry for her. For you are white and red, like a quite young piglet when it has just been born. Oh wife — oh shepherd — how happy I am, and how good the world is, and lovely creatures people are."

"Now come outside," the shepherd summoned Sophie assertively. And when they were both standing under the swishing November rain, the old man tapped his companion assertively on the arm, whistled his philosophical melody, and finally said very moment- ously, "From that, you can keep two things in mind now, my daughter. Firstly, only the stupid enter the war against habit. And secondly — and this is the key — an intoxication is always something beneficial, and is poured into men from above like a mild spring shower on the hard earth. For see, my daughter, some soil is so hard that without this gush, it would only give off pois - onous vapours. So an especially benign power had an insight and gave to men that which they cannot exist without. Namely, intoxication. And when a ground is so firm and dry that it no longer takes the natural things wanted by God, then you must just fetch an artificial aid. And that you will now always do, my daughter, with one and a half litres a day. No more. But then you will also see that it works like fine oil. The heavy, the so-called lovely properties which don't actually belong to it, they remain above; the base, however, and the coarse properties which make up the actual essence, they are suppressed, and sink to the bottom."

And as the wise man of Lower Pümplow thus spoke, it rang quaintly out of the cottage, and in full intoxica- tion of his soul, Martin Kriews, the eternally unemployed, sang his favourite song:

The Forbidden Intoxication

Man's highest happiness on earth
Is to loved and be loved.

THE FORBIDDEN MARRIAGE

"Shu-huch," the bellows hissed in the great village smithy of giant Tibäul, "shu-huch — shu-huch."

The fire sputtered, blue and yellow flames flared up like magical flowers which only bloom for a second, and then the iron chain of the bellows rattled again, for the mighty fist of the dark dread-locked Levin Tibäul was pulling on it while his left hand turned something white-hot back and forth amongst the charcoal.

"Shu-huch — shu-huch," the workshop's powerful chest breathed. Damp sweat dripped down the walls, and the entirely red bricked room immersed itself in the glow just like a forehead reddens from toil and work. "Shu-huch — now you think — ever think — shu-huch," it thus sounded.

In-between, however, the young smith roared from his powerful throat:

> My treasure, my child,
> I have never told you,
> You have a red mouth
> And a white knee —

Shu-huch — shu-huch —

> I am in love with thee.

"Kaboom," the heavy hammer smashed onto the anvil as if it had to thunder the bass accompaniment, and immediately the young smith cried out even more furiously as reinforcement to it:

> I am in love with thee.

"Well, now let it be," a rolling and growling voice soothed from the furthest corner, and father Tibäul, who was in that corner turning a crackling wheel hoop in the cooling tub. Gently and caressing just like he had stroked a blossoming cheek in his younger years, father Tibäul patted his giant leather apron, grasped at the same time his massively protruding hooknose, which peered down like a vulture from his primevally forested, grey-black shaggy beard, and opined blinking, "Well, now let it be, Vinny, I know all about that."

"How so?" the son shouted, and tore even more irritably at the chain. Shu-huch — shu-huch — "What do you know?"

"Well I know," the master affirmed slyly.

"You know nothing," the son refuted.

"Well, so I know nothing," the old man relented, nodding his head. "Let it be, Vinny. But tell me now, what sort of delicate thing are you actually working there?" with which he pointed with powerful fist at the furnace.

"That is a secret," Levin roared, and lowered his dreadlocks so low that his hair must now indubitably flare up in the embers. "A hidden secret it is."

"Good, if it is a hidden secret, then I don't want to watch any longer. Secrets must remain alone and in silence. But now look through the window, my boy, there comes a secret too, the head miller's only daughter, Ida — hello, with a proper bouquet of flowers in her hand. Also plucking secrets surely. Now, where did I get to? I was just saying, the miller Voss is a good man, a hard man, they are good people. Why not? I am also for secrets."

And with that, the old giant carefully opened the low side door, stooped low, and stepped out grinning, "Very good," he murmured softly to himself, "why not? It's a thing set aside."

***

Yes, there stood 'little Ida', as the miller Voss's only one was called, now under the half-open door of the smithy, holding the bouquet before her, and looking curiously at the activity of the young smith. Behind her, you could see a blue strip of sea running along, and the thin head around which the brown plaits coiled so pertly and self-assured contrasted cheerfully and full of light with this blue ribbon. But why does it remain silent for some time between them?

Who knows?

They are shy, feeling ashamed; and then again, the children of the north accept this eloquent silence, which knows how to talk so gently and intimately, lovingly into their hearts.

Thus calm reigned, only the sea wind pushed once against the door, rustled around the girl's skirt, and then travelled up the flue.

"Shu-huch."

Then the girl perked up, "Hey," she said, while she reached the bouquet out still further. "I'm here now."

"Yes," Levin grumbled through his teeth, averted, without seemingly noticing the girl or the bouquet.

She continued, "What was that song that you were singing before?"

"Song? — I don't know any songs."

"You do."

But suddenly the bellows whooped so that the fire blinked and flared up, and while the smith's assistant struck a formidable blow on the anvil, he stammered half to himself, "Hey, I made the song up."

"What?"

"Yes, I've often done such a thing."

When he had confessed this, the chain rattled again, a thousand red fiery roses whirled over the walls, and the formidable voice boomed half in shame:

My treasure, my child,
I have never told you,
You have a red mouth
And a white knee —

Shu-huch — shu-huch —

I am in love with thee.

Ka — boom — smashed the heavy hammer as if it had to thunder the bass accompaniment.

Then calm reigned again. The little flames sank down, but little Ida nestled her lowered head in her flowers. Her hand was trembling a little.

"That was pretty," she finally sighed after a while, whereby she attempted to lift her blue eyes, which seemed to be delicately stained by the smoke, toward the averted man. And after a pause, she added quite uncertainly, "Who did you make it up for?"

"Yes, for who surely?"

Then she stepped closer to him, "I have flowers here."

"So? Flowers?"

He squinted barely perceptibly to the side at the bouquet. The next moment, he was already raising with his tongs again a tiny, white-hot object out of the charcoal.

Then she tapped him gently for the second time on the shoulder, "It looks almost like a heart," she stuttered.

"Do you think?" he responded uncertainly.

"Who is it for?"

"Eh, it depends."

"Oh," she murmured, taken aback.

Then he made his artwork hiss in the cooling tub, fastened it to a quite fine steel chain which he had also made, and then stepped quickly up to her.

"There."

"What should I do?"

"Just put it around your neck."

And after the little iron heart rested on her, her breast rose and fell so quick and heaving, just as the bellows had been stretching itself before.

Shu-huch.

"Little Ida," Levin said, now thrown completely into confusion by her bewilderment, "I would like — I want — may I perhaps give you a tiny little kiss as a reward?"

She did not stir, shivered a little, and looked at him, "Yes, if you want to be so good," she finally replied, barely intelligibly.

Barely had it died away than he was embracing her exultantly with his sooty arms, and after she had held the bouquet right in his face for a moment as if in defence, she suddenly offered him her lips fully and without thinking.

"There."

"Oh God, thank you so much too," he stuttered blissfully. At that they began quite abruptly to dance around in the smithy until he lifted her slender figure up high to finally place her down carefully on the work table.

There she sat and dangled her little feet.

"Now you are my fiance, little Ida," he thus shouted as though possessed.

"What else? — Of course," she laughed. "Do you think that I would tolerate anything else?"

"God forbid — of course not," he roared, "and I will gift you everything now. Just pay attention. Aprons and rings and underskirts and a proper yellow canary."

"Yes, so it behooves," she endorsed, "and I will give you a kiss for that too. Only" — here she laughed brightly — "it's still funny."

"What, my dear fiance, my sweety?"

"Well that with the religions."

"What about religions?"

"Well, don't you know than? My mother is Catholic, and I am Protestant, and you? — tell me, is it really true then?"

"Yes," he stuttered, and stroked his chest uncertainly several times, "I don't know either, how it happens, but I am — —"

Then she hastily held his mouth shut, "Silently — I forgive you, if you are truly fond of me. Is that true, are you? The other thing we'll put right."

"Yes, Ida, there is no question."

With that he lifted her up once more, and this time he began to dance properly with her, an ungainly, festive waltz like people with such large feet perform. The unconstrained little thing, however, leant over his shoulder, and hummed cheerfully into his ear:

> My treasure, my child,
> I have never told you.

Then he belted out in answer to her, while he attempted to stroke her weak limbs with awkward fists:

> You have a red mouth
> And a white knee.

And then both together:

> Shu-huch — shu-huch, I am in love with thee.

Yes, to see such a couple was a proper and natural delight.

***

Only nevertheless — even though — meanwhile — sure enough — there were people who found this love union utterly unnatural. And there were three gentlemen whose views possessed an ignoble streak.

One beautiful morning, the vicar Friderici asked in fury of his housekeeper, Mrs Brandenburg, who kept the personal relations of his broad parish in order instead of his house, for his flock was only thinly sown and spread over six Pomeranian towns, "Tell me please, dear Brandenburg — apropos, the coffee smells excellent by the way, an admirable aroma — do you consider this misalliance, I mean this absolutely unfitting betrothal, really to be true?"

And when it was confirmed to him with mournful indignation, he then awkwardly shook the wavy locks which almost completely covered his tonsur and said, "Wonderful. *Roma nondum locuta est*[*]. We will have a word. Brandenburg, my coat, and Johann shall harness the horses immediately."

Thus spoke the vicar Friderici.

But quite close to the workshop of the unsuspected couple, Pastor Knaak rose up on the same morning imperiously from his mahogany desk, slapped his hands a few times angrily on the desktop, and finally collected his feelings in the exclamation, "Ridiculous, simply ridiculous. These reckless people will have to be talked into sense, or at least into making guarantees. Certainly! With the guarantees in this case, one will have to be content at worst. Sofie, my walking stick."

And so that the oldest and most select banner was also not missing from this religious campaign, the old Rabbi, Doctor Karfunkel, rose on this beautiful day of the Lord ill-temperedly from his bed in town, planted himself in deep thought before the white bed of his wife, and finally reasoned, scratching behind his ear, "You know what, Rosalie, it is afflicting me that human mild-heartedness, now, the mood shall we say, has subdued certain boundaries. Haven't we received a fat goose every year from old Tibäul out in Lower Pümplow about this time? Now, yes, we have no right to it. God forbid, not a shadow of a right. But yet, wasn't the goose like a beautiful sign of remembrance of that day when both

____

[*]   "Rome has not yet spoken".

the Tibäuls once stood before me at the altar. Should such relationships really be permitted to fall asleep? As I said, it is not because of the small advantage to me."

"It is," Rosalie contradicted him with displeasure, and sat up in her pillows. "You're saying it's so, with today's prices. And then, have you forgotten the beautiful lard that looked as white as freshly fallen snow?"

"Lard?" Doctor Karfunkel was unable to withstand this enticement. "Lard," he repeated, "now, as I said, this isn't about that for me. But look, Rosalie, I am anxious, I am anxious of temper about what is happening with old Tibäul. How can you know? With one of those great hammers, he could have smashed his hand or foot, or even his entire head. I consider it my human duty, I tell you, a quite urgent one, to look around after my people, and that I will do immediately."

Rosalie called after him, "But don't speak directly about the goose."

"Eh, what, I am only doing it because of the walk, and to inquire."

Thus the third banner was also drawn to Lower Pümplow. Only, when Doctor Karfunkel arrived at the smithy, he was informed that the father and son were to be found at the windmill of the miller Voss, where the betrothal of young Levin would be celebrated with all-round agreement.

"What a miracle! What betrothal?" the Rabbi started, whereby lovely pictures of entire streams of white glowing lard began flowing through his imagination. But suddenly he hesitated. "At the miller Voss's?" ran distrustfully through his mind. "How? For God's sake. They don't have to know. Or would those people act so modern and rebelliously? Fetch the killer of the goose. Why is my Rosalie always on about the goose? Here it's about the highest interests of mankind. Good God, all the things experienced in this modern world." With that he pulled the old, snug top hat down over his forehead, pressed the bamboo cane adorned with its golden button battle-ready into the damp soil, and hurried straightaway to the joyful betrothal, a high priest, fiery as the flames of the Lord. "Now, I will talk. I will tell them," he murmured to himself.

***

Meanwhile spirits are high in miller Voss's windmill. The great room on the ground level where the filled flour sacks were usually stored, is swept clean that day, and even the fact that, both on the walls and on the smooth floor, the traces of flour shine like freshly fallen snow, only heightens the general festiveness. They all sit there around the massive, round, yellow-flamed birch table, the couple, the parents on both sides, and the three mill servants, Klaus, Jochen and Stöffe, whose countenances also shine with flour and approval, and whose bodies almost already resemble, from the immensity of the festive breads consumed, the fully packed sacks of their employer.

"Cheers! Cheers!" Klaus shouts after every annihilated cup of coffee.

"Cheers!" Jochen answers on such opportunities, still swallowing.

"Cheers!" Stöffe joins in each time deeply stirred, while he offers his cup over to the miller's wife for a new fill.

Overall the general enthusiasm grows and swills. In particular, old Tibäul and the girl's father reside like friendly neighbours in each other's arms almost constantly, and every time the betrothed couple show each other some tenderness, then both fathers feel themselves obligated to confirm this likewise through a reciprocated kiss.

"How beautiful, when both our businesses don't abut each other," father Tubäul opines at the same time dreamily. "And the mill here, brother of my heart, should also be free of debts. Now, as I said, it is something set aside."

The eternally fidgety, tiny miller, however, springs around the table to answer, until he again lands by his heart's brother, whispering into his ear, "And your savings accounts in the town? Fine. I just say fine."

Whereupon the two allies kiss anew, while the miller's wife who has a tendency to be very melancholy and sentimental, regularly draws her handkerchief to soak up a few necessary tears.

"Cheers," Klaus murmurs, no longer able to hold his mouth open because of cakes.

"Cheers," Jochen concurs, chewing in competition.

"Cheers," Stöffe coughs, combining sweetbread, coffee, and emotion in his throat.

Oh, what a quiet, joyous, harmonious celebration.

Then the door creaks, and in the opening, a majestic, black-clothed figure appears, almost filling the entire frame.

"Isn't that?" miller Voss calls perplexed.

"Yes, certainly, it is the Vicar Friderici," the miller's wife leaps up, as she curtsies from fright and awe, so that her chair flies into the lap of the choking Stöffe. "Lord, the Vicar, what an honour."

"What does he want then?" miller Voss still has time to whisper to his other half.

This, however, is immediately clear. The Vicar approaches, and while he takes off his broad rimmed, black felt hat slowly and with a beautiful, measured movement, he looks around the cheerful circle gravely, but already gently reproachful, until his eyes meet with those of father Tibäul; then he shakes his head forbiddingly.

"Yes, my dear, good Mrs Voss," he begins, for the soul of this melancholy woman belongs solely to him, "I assume that you were awaiting me at such an important event as is about to be consummated in your family — for I hope it has not yet been consummated once and for all — is that right, I don't go astray in the assumption that you have surely expected me for a long time in these last, weighty and meaningful days of inner unrest in your soul."

Inner unrest of the soul? The woman turns red, stammers something, blinks at her fidgety husband, who is whipping his foot back and forth incessantly, and replies finally quite rudderless that she had surely, that is, she did not really know, and if the Vicar would be so good — to take a place — —

Again the Reverend shakes his grey locks with bitter repudiation, "My dear daughter," he ripostes somewhat stronger, "have you forgotten? At the time the Lord vouchsafed you this lovely blossoming daughter, did you not promise me then in a solemn, earnest hour, in a sense at confession — —"

"Come in!" miller Voss shouted.

"Come in," roared the three miller's servants after him, for this time the door had been knocked on with a powerful hand hard and energetically three times, and without worrying about another invitation, the tall, thin, blond Pastor Knaak hurried with firm, ringing steps in to the amazed company.

"Hello, my dear people," he threw out hastily while he hammered on the birch table nervously with his cane, as if his undertaking had to be dealt with in one minute. "Hello — hello," and then with a sudden recoil, "ah, faithful servant, Reverend. What a coincidence that we both meet."

"It is a pleasure to me," the Reverend slipped in with a little reserve.

"Yes — yes, certainly, I presume, though, Reverend, you are also appearing to —"

"What, what do you mean, Pastor?" the Vicar contradicted with his beautiful, majestic attitude. "I don't know —"

Only Pastor Knaak, filled completely with the categorical imperative and light, pure reason, in addition to being a disciple of Bismarck-like forewardness, does not think of delaying any longer with introductory words. Hastily, he strides up to the little miller, places both hands heavily on his shoulders to shake him strongly, as if he has to bring a besotted man a little to his senses, "But, dear Voss," he admonishes with his sharp military voice, "even if it is far from me to encroach in your personal affairs and sentiments, for you know it is the most important principle of our church to let our highest judge, thus the divine one, take as it were the bench in our own inner being — in this sense at least, Martin Luther pointed it out to us —"

Here the Vicar coughs, opens wide his great fiery eyes and begins to measure the preacher of this profession from top to bottom, "Hm," he clears his throat quietly.

But the zealous Pastor Knaak turns not a glance towards him. "You must not be offended, my dear miller," he continues, "but you have taken a step from the good path to salvation. For although I must concede that the smith Tibäul and those belonging to him are on the whole a family worthy of respect — I myself have just had the door to my pigsty recently strengthened by him with new hinges — it seems to me on the other hand very rash, unconsidered, and not handled very Christianly by you, to enter a close family alliance with confessors of an old, vanquished — yes — Mr Tibäul, I ask that you understand me correctly — even rough and bloody faith. And should one finally also defy this last, most extreme injunction, then a decision must be made in any condition by the young man present here who makes it impossible ...”

“Stop!” Vicar Friderici called out here, a strong wave of fervour having suddenly climbed up to his eyes. “Pastor, you perhaps do not know that an old, sacred promise of Mrs Voss here authorises me, no, truly, even obligates ...”

“What? How? Are you suggesting something, Reverend?” the sharp Protestant voice etches quite brusquely at this opportunity. “I thought I must at least attempt to make clear to our parishioner Mr Voss, undisturbed by Roman interference, that the voice of the Lord calls loudly through me —”

“Come in,” stuttered the three miller’s assistants, who had during this rising religious struggle been staring sorrowfully at the fine betrothal sweetbreads, “come in.”

In the doorway, someone bowed, but did not dare to approach this numerous gathering presently. “Forgive me, miller Voss,” apologised Doctor Karfunkel, at whom the other two clergymen stared, robbed of breath, even stunned, “I know I haven’t had the pleasure. I permitted myself only for the smith, Mr Tibäul — and because I did not find him at home, since a betrothal was to be celebrated here —” he took a step forward, fastened the old smith as well as the engaged couple searchingly in the eye, and rocked his head wistfully. “Now, I think,” he added with a reassuring smile, “it will have been a bad joke, and I would rejoice, dear Tibäul, if you were inclined to give me a little information about it, you know a quite private hint, in all amity. One would like to know something certain. Don’t you think?”

"Quite right, fully my view, something certain," his Reverend now called out, feeling, as almost always, stretched inwardly towards the representative of the most rigid principle, and at the same time, he planted himself battle-ready by the side of the Rabbi. "And hence I would like to remark straightaway, I in no way came here to somehow cause even the smallest difficulty for either of the dear families. For that, you are all far too magnificent and good people. Also of something rough or even bloody, of which the Pastor liked to speak before, I cannot with the best of wills discover the tiniest bit of it in the being of the Tibäul family themselves."

"Please, allow me," the Pastor interrupted here nervously, "how can you ..."

And Doctor Karfunkel also introduced something pitiful, yet very reproachful, "what do you mean, bloody? If that perhaps is an allusion —"

But the Vicar just laid his full, beautiful hand softly on his shoulder, and suggested winking, "By no means, my dear, revered doctor, in contrast. Do I not cherish for your character and your science, yes even for your entire culture, the greatest and most justified reverence of all? And if I allow myself to note something with this entire business which seems to bear such a beautiful and hearty impression, then it concerns merely the securing of certain promises which Mrs Voss here gave me once in a both painful and joyful hour." With full splendour and distinguished verve, as if an invisible Cardinal's train was dragging behind him, the Reverend then stepped before the young couple. "Yes, my dear children, I am placing nothing in the way of your love. Be just as happy as your hearts have harmoniously bonded, and in the name of an old plight, and for honour and safeguarding of our faith, which alone gives blessing, the only thing which I desire from you both, from you, young man, especially, consists in that the pledger of your future coexistence must be devoted to that comforting, all-forgiving faith which your mother-in-law here has adhered to since her childhood with all the intimacy of her soul."

Meanwhile, Pastor Knaak and Doctor Karfunkel had in silent facial expressions made understandable their divergent views of what had just been heard. But now the fiery Pastor Knaak could bear it no longer. Should one then always be knocked from the field by Roman exuberance and Jesuit diplomacy? "And where does the strict, moral claim lie?" he flared up in full fury. "What, future? I require, I demand with all determination, that if my agreement should in any way be desired and given, that the groom shall confess immediately to the confession of his bride. Doctor Karfunkel, I invoke you as a witness. Can you, venerable sir, think at all of a marriage founded happily in which both parties did not share a faith and a hope? Please, Doctor, answer me."

"He invokes me!" he resounded with quiet indignation towards it. "Now, there I must object, Reverend Pastor, where is it written, I ask where, that it must be only the confession of the young bride here which ...?"

Then the Vicar also discarded his measuredness suddenly, "Stop," he interrupted with a rising heat, whereby he grasped the Rabbi powerfully by the arm. "And I invoke you also as a witness, doctor. Haven't I exercised the most extreme self-restraint since I only occupied myself with the future? Did I desire perhaps a convert, as the Pastor thought to demand so self-confidently? By no means! Our demands are mild. They rest constantly on the quite precise knowledge of human life. I ask you, speak openly, my dear doctor! Judge entirely without prejudice. To which standpoint do you feel closer? Have the greatest confidence in me."

"Now, if I shall judge entirely openly, your Reverend," the Rabbi broke out now, his hands trembling with fury, "then I would like to be allowed to establish that it is actually our belief which possesses the oldest prerogative, strengthened by dear God himself. Have you forgotten what happened at Sinai amidst thunder and lightning? I am tolerant, now yes, I follow modern science, certainy, I am social, also good, but you must allow me when I am absolutely, fundamentally against all such intermarriages —"

He raised his arm high, moved it warningly in the air, and struck his chest loudly with his other hand.

"Yes," Pastor Knaak attacked here, tearing away, also lifting his arm, and moving his finger pontificating in the air. "You are right. No concessions, no half ways. Mr Voss, I ask you here for the last time. Will you succeed in drawing your future son-in-law over to you, or not? Woe to that man by whom the offence cometh into the world.[†] And if thy right eye offend thee, pluck it out.[*] Have you also considered that one day the dragon of re-morse could lift its head, and will then break you at the knees with inner reproaches? Have you considered everything?"

"Truly? Aren't you ashamed, smith Tibäul?" Doctor Karfunkel fell out of his role here without thinking, "aren't you ashamed that you are engaging in such an outrageous business? Is there not something great about the beliefs of our fathers? About the entirety of our institutions? Yes, even about being oppressed and subjugated? I tell you, Jehovah, despite all that, only has his pleasure in us. And you want to be so frivolous and resign your genuine, your old, your distinguished birthright for a pastry? Woe, how sorry you will be later."

"Pardon, what are you saying there actually?" here Vicar Friderici cut in with a haughty shrug of the

---

[†]   Cf. Matthew 18:7.
[*]   Matthew 5:29.

shoulders. "How can you, dear Rabbi, presume in our presence —"

"Admittedly, this tone of voice actually sounds very noteworthy," Pastor Knaak added with an ironic smile.

Only the bullet had been launched.

"What do you mean, presume? And why the tone of voice?" Doctor Karfunkel shouted, completely in the throes of his southern fervour, and this time forgetting all prudence. "Is this here not about one of ours? Do we live perhaps in the time of Torquemada in Spain? God forbid, one doesn't like to think of it in dreaming. How can the gentlemen, I ask of course with all due respect, forget so far as to simply repack someone of a different faith like wares in different paper? And then give it your stamp? Truly, an entirely new matter. Are there no Prussian courts anymore? I am only suggesting, your Reverend. I am only saying, Pastor."

But then something happened which none of the three spiritual commanders would even have anticipated.

The people rose.

With a sudden crack which made the windmill's walls reverberate, the old giant Tibäul sprang up, and smashed the coffee cup which he was holding just filled in his hand directly before the Vicar's feet. "Look," he roared, "Levin, that is a noble thing. Well? Did I put myself in such company here? Am I not the richest man in the entire village? And now someone wants to argue here over my dear, firstborn son? Voss, I ask you quite simply, is it now out of the question? Or becoming nothing? Then I'd a thousand times prefer to take my son back again."

"Excellent," said Doctor Karfunkel.

At this challenge, however, the miller sprang like a shuttlecock to his heart's brother, waved his hands about, and assumed a threatening pose. "What?" he

crowed, "did you hear, wife? A man who is actually des-
cended from a quite foreign, wild tribe, who does not
even want the honour of my daughter, of my flesh and
blood daughter? Eh, that would be a proper delight.
What a fortune that my eyes have been opened still in
good time by the religious gentlemen. But now it's over.
Entirely over. Now boil your lilac tea. I don't want any
more. I take my daughter back. My daughter Ida."

"But calm down, dear friend," the Vicar attempted
calmly to restrain him.

"Why will you engage yourself in such a thing?" the
Rabbi warned, shrinking back, while he attempted to
seize the old smith by a corner of his well-worn frock
coat.

Only all blandishments, every mediation, came too
late already. The smith struck out; it was as if a tele-
graph pole plunged swishing down on tiny Voss, and
then ...

"For God's sake, what have you perpetrated here?"
Pastor Knaak reprimanded the violent man. And when
the giant squinted with his bloodshot eyes to the side in
bewilderment, he saw with dull horror how the old
Rabbi crouched trembling on that chair on which he
had just then knocked him down by mistake with all his
strength. Copious blood was flowing from a cheek
wound.

With measured concern, the Reverend bent over the
wounded man. "Hopefully you haven't lost anything serious, my revered doctor?" he asked with his beautiful,
sonorous voice. Only the beaten man appeared genu-
inely petulant. "What would I lose?" he repeated with
bitterness. "You can believe me, Reverend, we simply
have a dark destiny. You might bicker with your gentlemen colleagues whenever you want and on whatever
period of world history soever, we have always taken the

beating. Well good, I'm not complaining, it is our destiny, but I tell you, my gentlemen, it is very painful."

***

And where were the engaged couple during all this?

The discord between the two heads of family had not yet fully lifted, the fathers were standing directly opposite each other still blustering and raving, when the young smith had forcibly taken his fiance away with him.

To where?

That he did not know. Only escaping that place where such desolate argument could open a gaping abyss around two lovers, around two lovers who had up to now only gazed joyously and lost into each other's eyes. Now they were stepping in turbid silence out into the solitary bright village street, across blossoming fields which shook their golden yellow heads in amazement at the couple, away over sprouting potato fields with their bluish flowers waving in the wind, all the way to the sea meadows whose damp, swampy ground smoked and fumed in the sunshine. Quite nearby, the still green sea was quivering. And strangely, did a flash or signal not come from there?

A signal too.

The girl perceived it first. She was powerfully startled by it so that the smith brooding to himself had to notice it himself. Instinctively he took her hand more firmly in his own, "What is it, my dear?"

Then she yielded to it falteringly and hesitantly. Did he not also think they actually possessed no place in the world anymore, and would it not be better if they were out there — at that she pointed at the wide, calm surface which shone across so sparkling and twinkling at them — would it not be better if they were both out there, closely entwined in each other — oh, he knew —

She faltered abruptly, sighed deeply, and her head sank heavily onto her chest.

"Yes, dear," her fiance answered firmly, although he dared not lift his eyes from the bright earth anymore, "dear, where you go, I will go with you too. I will not leave you anymore. But oh, what a pity —"

"What, Levin?"

"Look, I mean, we have probably come to each other too early, or even too late. What do you think?"

But she did not understand him.

And then they ran over the open fields blindly to the water so that the man's chest gasped and the girl's skirt swished and fluttered.

"What a pity," Levin thought once more at the lovely sound. But when they ran past the steep alder bush, little Ida seemed to have caught fatigue. At least she pulled up with rushing breath to lean heavily and deep in his arms, "I'm so tired," she burst out, "so terribly tired. Just rest for a little moment yet. Come, let's sit down."

Then he found likewise that their plan did not really need such haste, even that it was after all no longer all that important whether they remained a while yet together, or not. And didn't the little alder bush darken so autumnally red over the dried out ditch? And didn't the little, colourful goldfinch blare out so boldly and defiantly from its willow branch?

"Come," her fiance pandered, pained, "let's sit down again."

"Yes, Levin, for the last, the last time."

With difficulty, and barely understandable, she whispered her farewell to life. And so shaken did they both feel by it, that they sank into each other's arms to kiss away each other's tears.

"Adieu, Levin."

"Adieu too, little Ida."

"What a pity."

"Oh yes, quite a shame."

And then they kissed each other anew, and looked at the laughing sea, shaking their heads. But the sea wavered, trembled, and shook. Perhaps it was laughing too. Over what? Well, perhaps only over the trivial circumstance that on the other side of the alder bush, the old shepherd Sturm had been sitting since the grey of morning. With his blue knitted stockings and his profound, but practical philosophy, which could well have given good advice at that moment, and not taking the least notice either of the world-weary couple behind him. On the contrary, he continued knitting serenely, threw a look now, and then at his snuffling sheep, and then pondered peacefully again the scattered clouds rolling past above him on the blue heavenly canvas grazing in blessed calm.

"Woof," barked the vigilant Karo.

But quite close by, behind the alder bush, the girl huddled closer and more ardently to her chosen one, and breathed sobbing into his ear, "Oh, you my dearest — oh you my sweetheart — what a pity — what a pity."

"Yes, you my sweetie, you my love," chimed back trembling, "you are so soft and warm, such a pity, such a shame."

The shepherd continued knitting.

Then something could be heard rolling. Over the nearby country road, a wagon was travelling. It stopped, and when the shepherd looked up, he recognised the old Rabbi, Doctor Karfunkel, who, after he had arduously climbed down from his vehicle, strode towards him with an uncertain air. The preacher was holding his white handkerchief pressed against his cheek.

"Gentleman, aren't you bleeding?" shepherd Sturm called out while he rose respectfully, for he had had to drive some mutton into town for the Cantor of the cler-gyman, and hence knew him well.

"Well yes," the Rabbi replied, furrowing his brow, "what is it? It's a scratch. But if I am not mistaken, you make an excellent healing plaster, and I wanted just to ask whether —"

"Love to," the shepherd interrupted, the doctor could receive one right away, for he always kept them with himself.

"Very good," the preacher said.

He sat down next to the old man, and while the wound was now carefully cleaned and covered by him, Doctor Karfunkel could not contain himself from re-porting with presumptive casualness and inwardly blazing fervour his adventures in the windmill.

The shepherd swallowed. Then he laughed.

"What are you laughing for?" the Rabbi remarked discouraged. "What is there to laugh about? I tell you, it is a sorrow — and moreover, the couple shall be gone too."

"Gone?" The shepherd restrained himself, "Don't be offended," he said kindly. "For I am only a little man against such a learned doctor. But look, Rabbi," he ordered immediately, and pointed with outstretched hand at his flock, "would you please explain to me why there is only a black ram there, which does so much duty for the white ewes?"

Now Doctor Karfunkel threw an uncertain glance at his neighbour, then he rubbed his nose, and managed to be able to turn his head away as though by chance. It seemed as if the conversation was becoming unpleasant for him.

"What does this accident," he finally judged, "have to do with the unsuitable betrothal I informed you of? Apropos, did you not here a strange noise behind us?"

"Eh where, no, leave it," the shepherd hastily parried, "that is nothing. But now look how funny it is. Namely what the dear Lord is for us stupid children of men, whom I represent by this flock. And what you, and the Vicar, and the Pastor, and the police signify for us citizens, that my Karo signifies for the sheep. Obey, Karo, calm. And now do you see, Rabbi, how you now find that neither I, who am the dear Lord, nor my Karo, although he occupies here a sort of Commissioner's position, concern ourselves in the least with these love affairs between the two dissimilar sheep which play out quite brazenly in the bright light of day? And why not? Yes, look, preacher, first we delight in such a natural love which means for us in its beneficial consequences always a beautiful product. And secondly, we know quite precisely that our intermediation would come to nothing. For what impels my sheep to their choice must be ordered by one even higher than I am. You see, and then I prefer to be the good 'dear Lord', and sit here, and delight in it, and knit my stockings, and not split my head open over why it is just a black ram which gets along so well with the white sheep. Why should I? The two themselves don't know it. And then I should suss it out? I, who doesn't understand their language? — No."

The Rabbi rose quickly, "Good then," he gave his thanks, whereby he rocked his head a little embarrassed and condescendingly. "Well yes — that is a shepherd's standpoint. Why not? King Saul was also a shepherd. But thank God, we have progressed far in our culture since then. And against such rough instinctiveness, we are protected now not only by the law, but also by our high consciousness of moral standards. Now, I thank you, shepherd Sturm, I will show my appreciation from time to time."

With that he went away. The rolling of the wagon echoed on the white road. But why does the shepherd now sit and cackle so quietly to himself?

Why?

Perhaps he is delighting from a distance over the strong black ram and the saucy white ewe. Or is the old man listening perhaps to the sweet twittering of the colourful goldfinch which hops and woos, and woos and exults?

But perhaps it is not about any of this at all. In the end, the old man just listens to the strange life and jostle which is coming from the alder bush behind him, quiet, soft, almost lost, and yet it signifies life, the drive to eternity since the day the Father, God, formed the dust, smiling, and man appeared out of it.

"Oh, you my sweety."

"Oh, you my sole golden love."

And the knitting needles clattered, and the blue stocking trembled and danced in the air, and the corn field broke waves of ripeness and full splendour.

And look, the marriage was consummated there, in the name of God, the earth, and quite commonplace clear reason.

But the sea meadows donated incense, and the sunbeams danced a wedding reel, and the wind passed over the field, and roared from its powerful chest a liberating "Amen".

THE FORBIDDEN PLAY

Outside before the window, the snowflakes were ticking on the windowpanes, quite softly and delicately as if little white angels were going "tick, tick" with dainty fingernails, and as if in reply, the fire in the stove of the elegant bachelor's room then flared up.

It is the Sunday before Christmas.

"Good morning, Commissioner," the liveried servant wishes on entering.

"Morning, Friedrich — — well, what's new in the county?"

"Commissioner, Constable Böttcher awaits your command outside."

"Böttcher? So early on Sunday morning? What is it then?"

"Yes, he said he had confiscated a theatre bill."

"Man, what has he done?"

The Commissioner gets up from his chaise longue, on which he had been lying in his velvet morning suit, fumbles for his eyeglass and, when he cannot find it, begins blinking testily, "Listen, my good man," he recovered finally, "I hope you haven't understood the Constable correctly. Or are you thinking perhaps of playing a tiny little joke to get me going? Wonderful. Now, if I ask you though in all seriousness, what brings the Constable?"

"A theatre bill, Commissioner."

"Almighty."

In the meantime, Commissioner von Pitak has, however, found his monocle. He places it only to have it whir swishing on a ribbon around his little finger while he raises his expressive light blue eyes sanctomoniously to the ceiling, "Well then so, in God's name. Let him in." And with a deep sigh, he adds, "Seems again something new wants to enter my praxis, — come in."

It is a few moments later admittedly, when von Pitak has found out about the unbelievable, the "simply hideous" thing, from the mounted gendarme standing before him so martially and spur-rattling in his green uniform decorated with the white bandolier.

No, quite definitely, this Madame Sperling, the wandering theatre director who was permitted every year for three days in the marketplace of Granzin to put on a comedy in Schroder's hall — this artistic widow had obviously suffered a little damage to her "box of ideas".

"A world premiere, she advertises?" the Commissioner echoes still quite rigid with shock. And the Constable strokes his brown, closely shorn, chin beard to reply grumbling with displeasure, "So it states here, Commissioner."

"Well, there it shall though — give me the bill once more, dear Böttcher. What's the thing called?"

"At your command, Commissioner, it is called 'The Consequences of Love'."

Now the Commissioner strikes the table with his hand so that it rings, "Well, so the Sperling woman must have turned right bad. Consequences of love? No, listen, dear Böttcher —" At this the Commissioner has sprung up, and now drums about on the firmly frozen windowpanes, "I am certainly amiable and don't like to make unnecessary unpleasantness. But consequences of love? No, no, that simply won't do. What is the woman actually thinking?"

And suddenly he turns around sharply, and tosses out curtly, "Tell me please, by whom incidentally is the concoction?"

At this question, however, the bearded gendarme's head must first dip down again into the bill before it can reply.

"By a certain Florian Otto, Commissioner. This Florian, however, is also participating. It states here. 'A young Count — Mr Florian Otto.'"

"Count? Aha —" The Commissioner smiles with irony. "Probably molesting the nobility again. That is the trump now." And after a while, von Pitak inquires more in-depth as to whether a woman did not also belong to this Count.

"Yes, Commissioner, it's printed on a line underneath. In bold. Clare — but written with a-i."

The Commissioner nods, "French," he opines, "that figures. She wants now to signify by that such a rotten character from the outset. Well, and who plays this Claire?"

"An Anna Krethlow."

"Krethlow? — Krethlow?" von Pitak gazes at the tips of his patent-leather boots. "Wait, where have I heard that name before? I must know."

Now the Constable allows himself to rattle more distinctly with his spurs in answer, whereby he places his finger on the seam of his trousers.

"At your command, Commissioner," he recalls, "that is the name of the baker at the market in Granzin."

"Correct — Krethlow," his superior becomes bouyant, "one of our best taxpayers. I would be sorry if perhaps some relationship —. Well, now listen please, Böttcher. The matter stands like this. If Sperling has presented her play as per regulations to the mayor Mengdehl, then the matter no longer lies in our department, then 'The Consequences of Love' can also leave us quite cold. Understand?"

"At your command, Commissioner."

The Commissioner strokes his blond moustache. "If it would also be best for us," he continued, "in confidence, to flag the thing of art to the raging bulldogs, it does not suit my taste at all. I am myself much too great a friend of the theatre, and over this, this Madame Sperling — well yes, a very pleasant and nice woman. If I had not been occupied again today by this mandatory orgy in the soldiers's club, truly, the matter would be immediately sorted in person."

With that he strode quickly through the room a few times, until he finally stopped with a firm resolve before the Constable, "Well then, as I said," he concluded finally, "if the mayor has accepted this piece of art, *tant mieux**. If not, yes then" — he shrugged his shoulders — "then I'm sorry, Böttcher, then you must just ride to the Sperling woman to inform yourself about the content of the play on the quiet. Understand?"

"At your command, Commissioner."

"And as you already know, if in the thing such rotten stories occur which you cannot put before a young girl, then give the Director my regards and tell her it pains the Commissioner, but she must play something else this evening. The Maid of Orleans or Faust. After all, they would also be plays that concern the consequences of love. — So, and now be delicate with the matter, dear Böttcher — goodbye."

***

The snowflakes were whirling thicker and wilder, and when the wind howling through the narrow lanes chased the white powder through the dark gateway of Schroder's inn, two young children who remained there closely huddled up trembled as though chilled, and instinctively snuggled up warmer and more compactly together.

---

*   "so much the better".

She was a strikingly pretty, young blond with a pert snub nose, who now looked up helplessly at her companion, a tall young fellow with black, wild strands of hair, very red hands and a clean-shaven face from which a pair of watery blue eyes looked out at the world in great awkwardness and as though pleading for forgiveness. It was also quite unfavourable for the first lover of the Sperling troop — namely with regard to the prevailing coldness — that his trousers did not reach entirely over his boots.

He plucked at them from time to time, only it was no help, they did not intend falling any lower.

"Must I go in?" the girl inquired, looking around hastily.

"Not yet," the youth reassured, shaking his black strands of hair while his tenuously thin body turned in its narrowly pinched Prince Albert coat with its wafting tails, and stooped, "Not yet, my sweet treasure. The Director has her fairy scene first."

"Oh, Florian —"

"I hear you, my love, my sweet child."

Woosh — woosh — a new wind gust blew through the gateway so that the lover had to stamp his feet from the chill.

He was wearing yellow summer boots. It was probably in keeping with the role.

"Oh Florian —"

"Speak, my everything —"

She grasped his hands, but immediately drew her fingers away again shocked, shivering from this living icicle, "Do you think he will come?" she whispered in feverish tension, "quickly, say."

The youth looked at her trembling, red lips, and bent down closer to them, drawn as it were by these cherries in the snow.

"Our hope remains," he responded with dullly rolling emphasis. "It is our fate."

For a while, it was silent, only the powdered snow crumbling glittering over the cobblestones of the entrance, and the gates groaned and creaked.

"Oh for a glass of grog," the lover thought disjointedly, while behind the white girl's forehead, next to misfortune, fate, and sorrow, the enlivening stimulus of red mulled wine began to blaze up.

"If it were only a single little swallow," she murmured, oblivious to everything around her.

"What?" The youth rubbed his red hands together. "Did you say something, my love?" he stuttered.

"Me? — No, I just thought about if he had refused. Oh, think, if he stayed away now. Oh God."

"Yes, that would be unthinkable," he admitted sombrely. His eyebrows knitted together darkly, and his head bent like a wilted lily. "Unthinkable," he continued, but suddenly he pulled himself up from his cold horror once more, "Haven't I — assuming his appearance — prepared everything for his final softening? Can you really doubt, you dear creature, that he could resist the great close to the third act — no, conceal nothing from me."

"Certainly," she stammered, swaying, "it seems very poignant when I kneel down so." Only straight afterwards, an ugly thought seemed to wrinkle all the flowers again in her little garden of hope. "But he had night-work today with his assistants," she stammered, appalled, "did you forget that? And then —"

"Yes, then admittedly," and at the same time, he stretched his right hand out with a lost, dismissive gesture, "Then —"

"Oh, it would be too ghastly," she softly groaned, and genuine, real tears ran over her blooming cheeks, "then we would never get together; for without his blessing, you know — and entirely without wreath and the Pastor —” oh, she shivered within in — “never, never.”

Again he lowered his sombre brow, and this time, it was driving fear which shook his voice along with his trembling body, “certainly, he still exercises the paternal power over you, and such fatherliness, my sweet beloved, bestows rights on the man concerned, which —”

Then he was interrupted.

Light hoofbeats were approaching from the street, and in the next moment, a broad, portly gendarme’s figure rode in the gateway, which was too low to receive this towering guest. The rider had to stoop so that the spike on his helmet would not be stripped by the protruding girders.

Now the green uniformed man stopped, and moved his foot a little in the stirrup as a sign that a greeting would be appreciated. When it wasn’t forthcoming, however, the white-gloved fingers first tapped soothingly on the neck of the whinnying stallion to then straightaway draw from his tunic a thick notebook with which a firmly detaining gesture towards the concerned couple was immediately executed.

“Morning,” rang down powerfully from above. “Drama is being acted here.”

“Indeed.” The lover attempted to strike a pose, which his frost-shaken body did not particularly support.

“So?” An inquiring look from above, “Do you belong to that?”

“Certainly.”

“Aha.” — The notebook was briefly scrutinised.

“Named Florian Otto? Well?”

God, what is it? The couple recoiled in shock, and if the narrow door of the inn had not opened at the same moment, and a thick beery, sticky voice croaked out to them, “Krethlow, where are you hiding? Make legs, girl — the old woman is raging,” this incident would not have occurred; quite certainly, the small blond would have fallen under the hooves of the stallion from shock and fear. But she was seized by the thick, swollen hand, and conveyed without delay or delicateness through the crack in the doorway.

"Oh God" her shaking voice faded away. Then her lover found himself alone with his mounted harrasser.

"Well, listen," the latter began now with displeasure from the height of his stallion, "you're enacting something nice here."

"Me?" Florian turned bright red, and brushed his hand through his streaming hair. Great God, what did this man seem to be confiding to him? "Oh, please," he fended with downcast eyes, "please, nothing has taken place."

"Well, let that be — it's all over — we've investigated already."

"On my word of honour," Florian cried now, holding firmly to the wall glistening with ice, for his legs would not carry him any longer. Ha — now the end neared, the long awaited. The hostile power was moving towards his decent and honourable body, and wanted to befoul it.

"My fiance is an undefiled rose," he murmured half benumbed, and thought he had said something noble and chivalrous, but this declaration of honour seemed to exercise only a very small impression on Constable Böttcher. What was concerning him? Fiance? Good — these actors possess many fiances. What else? — But the play — what was it called though? — Right, "The Consequences of Love" — a piggish title — ugh, disgusting —. The play had not been submitted to the mayor as per regulations — no trace of a due process — and for that reason must not be performed according to Paragraph 218, Section Two of the Public Safety regulations.

"Simply not performed, my dear."

"Constable," the lover cried, instinctively throwing his hands up high in the air as if he were a messenger of misfortune in a Greek choir, "Say 'no' — that you are not serious."

"So?" the rider shook his bearded head in astonishment, "listen to me, please, we do not joke in uniform."

"Good heavens — I am lost."

"Eh, pranksters, then just perform something else. It doesn't matter."

"But, the play is by me."

"Well now. Why did you write such a thing? Such a questionable story."

"Enough — enough, Constable — only the henchmen of power judge thus —"

"What? — Eh, that is jealousy."

The Constable suddenly swung his right leg with a flamboyant rider's motion from the saddle, dismounted, and now stood weightily and spur-rattling next to the thin youth, like an oak tree next to a trembling bean stalk, "You, listen," he now began very determinedly, while he stroked his chin beard, "Do you know something new? In the entire matter, something doesn't agree. Now kindly come into Schroder's bar, we want to talk about this together a bit more. Right? — Yes, always lead the way."

With that he slung the reins of his horse around the gate, buckled his sabre somewhat lower, and grasped his pistol holster as if he had to be armed and ready for all situations. It was, however, turning green before the lover's eyes. In a half unconscious state, as if he were swaying through a black dream, he floundered into the barred off, brownishly smoky bar, and when he had settled down at a round table covered with a colourful oil cloth, he absentmindedly ordered two pints of beer from the small, loitering barman. He could also have demanded mustard or ox blood, his soul dwelt so completely in other dimensions.

Beer — mustard — gall. What did it matter? But his love, had she not just now been strangled by a pair of rough fists in white suede gloves, and thrown into the grave? Oh what horror lurked in these dark hours.

And the haze danced ever greyer and more insubstantially around him. And strangely, was he in fact still himself crouched here opposite the Constable who had spread his legs with their top boots so meaningfully before him? Was it really the lover Florian Otto who had to answer so unresistingly to suspicious questions, recognising that he had not been christened in the cradle Florian, nor Otto, but was called August? Simply August Fuhrmann from Malchow? Yes, a few months ago, thus concluded his incomprehensible confession, he had still been a clerk — well yes, shop assistant if nothing else — with the merchant Bolljohann in Stralsund, from where, however, he had been driven away by the fierce urge of art.

"Well, listen, Fuhrmann," the Constable interrupted, taking notes zealously, "then you are thus in your beliefs a quite commonplace materialist?"

"Oh no, I have always been for Schiller."

"Well, let it be, that is surely just so much sophistry which would add to the obscurity. Well now but, my dear man, to the essentials. How did you actually come to be travelling around here under a false name? You know also what that means?"

Florian clasped the arms of his chair. Now he would not be surprised anymore if his four legged seat had suddenly transformed into the massive stallion of the gendarme to sit with him whinnying over the table, "False name?" he stuttered, "that — that — allow me, — that is just a custom of artists — quite harmless."

"So? Harmless?" Böttcher repeated while he wiped the beer from his beard with his red handkerchief. "You are a fine one. Do you also know that I recently placed just such a one as you in handcuffs out in the open? — And then two steps ahead and into the county prison? — What do you say to that?"

"Oh, but not — but not."

"Well, and you probably haven't registered either? Well?"

"No — no."

"You, there is something fishy with you though," the Constable suggested threateningly while he slapped his notebook on the table, "who knows what sort of profile has been left all behind you."

And as much as the crestfallen lover now also begged and adjured that it must be a misunderstanding, and how everything would be explained, the gendarme maintained that such breezy customers all said that, and the inquiries would result in further things.

In this moment, gentle tones penetrated through the closed door to the hall. Bright women's voices were singing. Gentle and full of acquiescence. It was the closing song of the blessing fairies from the "Consequences of Love".

> Love must be possessed by the man
> Who wants to wander the earth.
> When fury and rage heat us up,
> Love makes us still again.

Then Florian pointed with outstretched arm to the near door, behind which his poetry was just then ringing out poignantly.

"That is by me," he said with broken pride.

"Yes, still — yes, still —", he breathed it in, "love makes us still again."

The gendarme raised his eyebrows, and tapped loudly on his hefty thigh. The power of the notes also seemed to have attuned his stalwart disposition milder, "Listen, Fuhrmann," he began in astonishment, "that last bit was not so stupid at all." He scratched for a moment thoughtfully in his smoothly parted hair. "Well, then enough of that," he finally blurted out decisively. "Then give me, please, a short overview of what occurs in your theatrical story, just what happens, I mean. But short, and the whole truth."

Oh, you dear, kind God, a ray of hope is beaming here. The fiance and the play and the poetic fame, yes, physical security itself, everything could still be saved. And so the man being interrogated then explained, and it sounded almost like a fairy tale.

Once upon a time there was a very, very virtuous, wondrously beautiful daughter of a master craftsman, and she had been filled with fervent desire for the colourful lamps of the stage. Then a young Count with lots and lots of money came, and abducted the young girl from her cruel father.

"Abducted?" the Constable cried, furrowing his brow. "Well, listen, you aren't serious about that?"

But it would have been a quite virtuous, high-minded abduction, Florian attempted timidly to sanitise it. But the Constable dismissed these objections angrily.

"Eh what, anyone can say that afterwards, the essential thing remains — but tell me the whole truth —" at the same time, he drilled through his opposite with a penetrating police look. "Are the two travelling together now? I mean quite alone and without guard? And then? Understand —" he winked, "have the two then perhaps lived together in a room in a hotel? But please, without excuses."

He had passed over that without a hint, the lover stammered, again very depressed.

"Aha," the Constable laughed scornfully, "then we have the thing, then we have it by the right corner. Aren't you ashamed, my dear man, to want to place such smut before our respectable and well-mannered female public in Granzin? But now stop. Nothing will come of the matter at all. The entire story seems rotten to me."

"But, I beg you," the poet cried in despair. "The chasing father gives his forgiveness at the end, induced by the song of the fairies."

"Eh, yes, doesn't fit him at all. A proper father, even more one who plies his respectable craft, never takes such wares back again afterward. You can bank on it that you don't understand."

"But allow me please —"

"No, that is it now, I won't allow it, it's forbidden, you here, my good man, are expressly forbidden by the authorities. And because of your particulars, please come to our office tomorrow for a bit. There I would like to introduce you to my County Commissioner so that he can also have the pleasure. So, and here is the money for my pint of beer, for we don't let ourselves be influenced in official business, understand? There you don't know us well. Bye."

He sprang up, straightened his legs, covered his head with his spiked helmet, and was thinking to leave the smoky premises just then with martial decorum when his intention was delayed and confounded by a quite strange sight. With his last words, in fact, the door to the hall had opened, and in her fairy costume, consisting of a low cut, golden glittering bodice, as well as a muslin skirt strewn with silver stars, which revealed strangely red tights, Madame Sperling, the director, had then entered, and her fluttering brown eyes, which formed a strange contrast with her golden blond hair, had immediately recognised the threatening situation.

"For God's sake" — that was the first thing which passed through her mind — "and the hall was almost sold out for this evening." No, under no circumstances, such a dark plan would have to be countered. Quickly, as if she had been smitten by feminine shame before the staring eyes of the Constable, the fairy threw a cloak over her shoulders, and then flew at the official as if her best acquaintance was unexpectedly and incomprehensibly thinking of scurrying away from her threshold, "But, my dear Constable," she encouraged with her bright voice, while she rattled the heels of her gold lacquered shoes up and down flirtatiously before the official, "you will not do that to me, hurrying away from me without a single greeting? No, that is not right at all. And in addition, as I hear, you have just now had a little difference with the first lover of my troop" — she made a gesture of introduction with her little, white hand — "I don't know whether the gentlemen are already known to each other, Mr Florian Otto, a quite distinguished mem - ber of my institute, Constable — —" she faltered.

"Böttcher," the gendarme finished, completely taken aback by this formality.

"Certainly, certainly," the Director cried with her most silvery laugh and a teasing, mischievous arch of her eyebrow towards the disconcerted man. "How can you think that such a name would be unknown to me? No, sir, we all know you here quite excellently, and for a long time, your loyalty to duty and policing efficiency has been described to me from the most various sides famously. But now I ask you, revered Constable — —" at this point the cloak was displaced quite by chance, and the golden glittering fairy bodice surfaced fleetingly again — "but now, my dear Constable, you must abso - lutely give me quarter of an hour in my room, for I have the most important disclosures to submit to you, both over my business operation, and also over the play being performed this evening, 'The Consequences of Love', disclosures which your head chief, the County Commissioner von Pitak, whom I know very well, must certainly also be extremely interested in."

And miraculously, before the Constable could settle seriously into defence, for the famed loyalty to duty of the well-tried official admittedly intended this, a round, plump arm had already nestled under his, and extremely astonished over himself, the gendarme saw how he led the glittering fairy away, first from the bar, then over the frosty gateway, and finally up a narrow, winding, wooden staircase to a small, comfortable room in which books, reels, and the most colourful masque clothes lay in confusion everywhere. Then he had to sit down, he indeed did not want to, but two little hands pressed the strong man down, and finally he heard nothing but a nimble little chatterbox beginning to chat at rushing speed about the business operation, the audience, the performers, the play, and in particular about the box office takings.

"Yes, Constable," she opined to conclude somewhat slower, "if a prematurely widowed woman like I should manage all this, she should indeed not have to face any unnecessary difficulties."

"No, no, Madame," the gendarme now replied noticeably more subdued, "the County Commissioner suggested the same."

"Yes, that I believe," the Director pondered to herself thoughtfully. "Mr von Pitak is a gentleman through and through."

"Well, and now listen please," the Constable continued alertly, "I would not have thought that your stuff would reap so much. But as the accounts prove, you stand there quite lightly. Listen, it seems wonderful to me though. And you carry all that out so entirely alone?"

"Yes," the delicate Madame Sperling confirmed, and looked at her visitor suddenly quite wide-eyed and as though stunned by an inner intuition, "entirely alone, my dear, revered Constable. Who would surely help me with it?"

"Well, tell me please, do you not have one of your actors who could give you a hand for a bit?"

"From this cast?" the fairy asked, doubtful over it, and sadly drew her cloak back from the red tights. "Oh, if you knew, Constable, how difficult it is for a woman to maintain the most necessary order among such people."

"Yes, of course —", here Mr Böttcher seemed carried away, "the right breeding is probably missing in the band. Well, listen, Mrs Sperling, it must, however, be able to be got right as it were."

"Yes, anyone who understands it well," she responded softly while her golden bodice sparkled.

"Her visitor rose and, becoming quite warm, tapped with his fist on the account book of the Director. "Well, and you believe," he said with his powerfully commanding voice, "that if the thing here is carried out tightly, the income could yet increase?"

"That could be confidently assumed," Madame Sperling confirmed, and she folded her hands as though discouraged. "For understand, my revered Constable, in such business as my own, it depends less on aptitude and talent than on commanding and obeying. But how should a delicate woman obtain these qualities? From where? I ask you."

"Thunderbolts, Madame Sperling," the guest now boomed, and stroked his stiff moustache with a brisk elan. "If it merely depends on that — and all the rest takes care of itself, then I think — — — well, as you said," he threw a scrutinising look at the resting woman leaning so completely unsuspecting and busy with herself in the ripped cane chair. And suddenly he dared to stroke with his white gloved fingers, which usually kept watch so stringently on the law, quite gently and soothingly over the white female shoulder from which — by chance — the cloak had fallen. "If it merely depends on that, well then, Director, you should not give up hope. It is not yet evening. You are also quite right, such a woman should not be presented with unnecessary difficulties — precisely that in fact were my instructions. And do you know what I'll do now before we discuss any further? Now I'll ride first and foremost to the baker Krethlow at the market, whose appearance you make so much of, and bring the old grouch. Such conveyances I understand. The man has nothing to laugh about. Till later, young woman."

He placed his hand on his spiked helmet, and struck his heels together as he had previously only ever practised as an Orderly for his commanding General. Thunderbolts yes, this Mrs Sperling, an exceptionally nice and strapping woman. With her you could have a go at the matter. Well, then to mount up, and go to the baker Krethlow.

***

This theatre evening was never forgotten in Granzin. If older residents still speak of it today, then they rock their heads dreamily, and suggest that such exquisite, touching artistic pleasures are simply unable to be given anymore these days.

Yes, yes, at the time when Anna Krethlow played Claire, and a lover stood by her side to whom at the first moment every girl in Granzin's heart flew.

Yes, that was art.

"Do you still remember surely, mayor Mengdehl? Do you still think about it, my dear Mrs Quast?"

"Yes, yes, it was so. There sat the old fat master baker Krethlow in his white work jacket right up front in the packed hall, in the first row, and next to him was seated the Constable Böttcher who from time to time threw a subduing look at him as if he had to keep watch on a dangerous criminal. And at the same time, the old grouch behaved quite calmly in the first two acts. And when he waved his hands about occasionally somewhat excitedly, the official sitting next to him could only vaguely understand what the offended father was murmuring to himself, 'It's nice — yes, yes, so it is. Haven't I always said? Well, let it be, let it be.'

But then, then the great moment turned up, that moment which acted just as unforgettably. The chasing father had just appeared on stage, that fat, bloated figure which the blusterer operated at the time for Madame Sperling, and he had just raised his hand to curse.

Then it happened.

Mayor, was that stirring or not? And how you cried at the time, Mrs Quast.

For suddenly, suddenly — oh, every heart faltered — suddenly Anna Krethlow, the ravishing blond actress, threw herself about with streaming tears, and while she stretched out her beautifully formed arms to the first row, she suddenly screamed with an urgent voice, 'Father, forgive me!'

For a moment, a deep, breathless silence. Then it went through the hall, 'Look — look — listen — what did she say?'

'Father, forgive me!' rang out even more urgently for a second time.

'Bravo! Bravo!' roared though the hall, and men and women rose, and clapped their hands. 'How stirring,' they whispered, 'the way she says it — no, now he must forgive her.'

'Did not cross my mind at all,' the old master baker grumbled under his breath. 'Was I asked before? But now there is a great hole there. Now I should stuff it, what? Eh, what will I do then? So stupid.'

'Father, forgive me!'

And now the lover also threw himself down next to his beloved and also stretched his hands with a really compelling movement out towards the implacable man. 'Father, forgive her!' he cried sobbing. 'You must — you must, I alone am guilty.'

'So?' the master baker now sprang up furiously, 'have I stirred your soup? Now eat it up alone. Eh, that would be nice.'

'Forgive, forgive,' roared through the hall. 'Anna Krethlow, hooray! Hooray, master baker Krethlow —' — 'Calm, he is an old grouch. Quiet, play on.'

But in this precarious moment, the beautifully painted rear door opened, and in danced the Director herself in her golden glittering fairy costume, and the redemptive song rang out now melodiously and full of acquiescence:

> Love must be possessed by the man
> Who wants to wander the earth.
> When fury and rage heat us up,
> Love makes us still again.

'Yes, so you say, Director,' the master baker called out furiously. 'Have you perhaps valued the child as much? And then the disgrace? Eh, then I must be not right in the head.'

'Father, forgive me!'

'Thunderbolts, most revered, just forgive her,' a very bright voice suddenly mixed into this dramatic dispute. And when the public rose curiously, it recognised with reverential astonishment that the County Commissioner von Pitak was looming in his tail coat and decorated with medals quite unexpectedly next to the seat of the old grouch. The high official had a short time before left the orgy at the soldier's club extremely enlivened and joyous from champagne, and had in passing by arrived at the idea of satisfying himself over the mission of his Constable.

Now he took the leading role in this end game.

'Commissioner,' the master baker stuttered in confusion as he rose waveringly, 'are you serious? Are you really, heartily serious?'

'Father, forgive me — father, forgive her.'

The Commissioner bent forward, and set his absolutely necessary monocle before his twinkling blue eye. 'But, my good man,' he broke off fiercely, 'that is a quite superb girl. An unusually endearing appearance. Of such a daughter, you can be directly proud.'

'Hooray! Commissioner von Pitak!' the public cried, 'hooray! Anna Krethlow — forgive, forgive.'

The old grouch scratched his head. 'Well, if the Commissioner really thinks so,' he finally pulled himself together uncertainly, 'well, then be quiet, Anna, let it be, I will then again. And your beloved, I'll accept him too. He can enter my house. And you, Director, I'll pay for the severance of both.'

'Yes,' the gendarme agreed approvingly, 'there must be a severance payment. The regulations require it.'

'Father, father! Thank you, thank you!'

And the Director had to come forward once more to give the closing song for their benefit, which was very well received. And it was a perfectly uplifting celebration in the antique sense, for not only on the stage, no, also in the public, the verses of the poet Florian Otto were sung with enthusiasm:

> Love must be possessed by the man
> Who wants to wander the earth.

'Bravo, bravo! Hooray, Commissioner von Pitak! Hooray, Director!'

When fury and rage heat us up,
Love makes us still again.

Yes, it was a glorious evening. Do you still remember, mayor Mengdehl? Do you still think about it, my dear Mrs Quast?"

Such exaltation does not happen anymore, for the hearts do not beat so simple and warm anymore, and the times have become more demanding.

But the Commissioner von Pitak experienced a special surprise just as he was wanting to climb into his coach, whose door was held open for him obligingly by Constable Böttcher.

"My goodness, Böttcher," he turned around astonished at the news which sounded quite whimsical to him. "You are marrying the Sperling woman?"

"At your command, Commissioner."

The Commissioner opened his eyes wide, and pushed his elegant top hat back a little. "Listen," he finally decided, "that — that comes as quite a surprise to me. But in any case, your future wife is in every respect an industrious woman. Without a doubt. Well, and you know how to be a correct Prussian constable who finds his way ultimately in everything. Even in artistic matters. Will bring traction to the band and give the entire business greater discipline. And now give your fiance my regards, and convey to her, she would know already, I have always maintained that the most unpredictable thing on our splendid planet remains once and for all the consequences of love. So, and now good night, Böttcher."

The horses drew away, and the Commissioner went away from there.

Yes, it was a glorious evening.

Now the curtain has fallen; and those who performed at the time are all gone. For this is a story from my childhood.

CHRISTIN DÖRTHE'S ENGAGEMENT

"Yes," Ott Boll said to Christin Dörthe, next to whom he was crouching on an overturned boat quite close to the edge of the green sea meadow, "today there's good weather for it."

"What do you mean by that, Ott?" Christin inquired, whereby with her rough, bare foot, for she was a strapping, tall girl, she pushed her clog back and forth through the damp grass a bit. "What do you mean by that?"

"Yes," he began again, scratched his bristly, blond hair self-consciously, and then stared at the nearby beach boulders between which green furrowed little riverlets rippled wearily to and fro, "Yes, I mean for getting engaged. Around Pentecost is the best time for it."

"Yes, do you want to then?" she wondered, as she turned her broad red face to him in astonishment, and at the same time, she fingered her thick, blond plaits a little.

"Yes," he murmured, "I want to."

"Yes, but Ott Boll," she objected, "you have though — —"

"Eh quiet, girl, quiet, I know everything, you think I had something as a sailor with the beach warden's daughter up in Ölland; but — —"

"So? Did you have something?" his tall companion interrupted him, and looked calmly at him.

"Yes, but," Ott apologised, "if the little child afterwards is from me, that the court up there won't be able to figure out."

"Well, then it's all good so far, I mean just —"

"Stop," Ott Ball cried, and struck is fist against the eroded keel, "I know everything, you think I was the one who cleaned out the merchant Raßmusen's store? But Christin, can anyone prove that? Didn't the Chief Justice rather say to me in particular, 'We hereby acquit you, but you must never do it again either'?"

"Yes, I know that well, Ott. But that is all no use, it is definite — —"

"What? What? What?" Ott cried, and turned quite pale in his bloated round, plump face. "Oh, you are surely thinking of the stupid story with the wife of the smoker Rupps? Look, I would have held you to be cleverer. Can I say something perhaps about that? She is in her forties now. And then with the old woman! Look, I'm walking past the old smokehouse quite calmly, and there the old woman stands before the door, and calls me in as she explains her man isn't home, and whether I might take the smoked eel from the smoker? Now, why not then? I'm a helpful fellow. So I climb up into the flue, and as the smoke is biting into my eyes, she grasps me below by the sock and says there's a hole in it. She wants to patch it for me. Now I don't otherwise have a loving hand in God's world for such things; so I say 'yes', and after I have brought down the smoked eel for her, I sit down before her, take my sock off, and she patches it. But what did the devil have planned for me? Then the accursed thing, the other sock, also had a hole, and in the end, the entire sordid, irksome trousers too. Should I perhaps have let the fitting opportunity slip? — No, nobody could want that. And now I ask you, Christin Dörthe, how can I help now that Madam Rupp's husband comes straight home, and sees me sitting there so? It was a great misfortune for me, and I also then only knocked out his two front teeth out of pure decency and sympathy for the poor woman. So, now you know my innocence."

There Christin Dörthe laughed so brightly, and then she burst out a little slyly, "Yes, Ott Boll, do you think then?"

"What? What?" the fatty blustered in fury, "is there something else? You're really picking on me though. Oh then, I know everything. You mean that stupid old story, when they found me that time stiff and thin before Klaus Dudy's door? But now Klaus Dudy too. He is such an old Venetian, such an old stealthy one. There he comes, the old sneak, straight along the bulwark. Look, girl, with Klaus Dudy, you don't let yourself get involved by any means, he's a fine one. Listen. Then he calls to me that time from out his window that I should come in, he had received a quite new medicine from an old shepherd which would make you live a long time. I look at the thing, what is it? — blackcurrant wine. Look, Christin, and half an hour later, I lay there under his window, and was dead. And what had the hound poured into me? Well, what do you probably think? Undiluted spirits. And that shouldn't be taken by men! So, but, girl, now you know me inside out, and now I want to ask you here on this boat in all solemnness — —"

Only the sailor did not finish this time either. For Christin Dörthe did not hide her rough, brightly ringing laughter at all, but slapped her chest with her hand, and cried aloud, "Stop, Ott, just stop, you never let me get a word in. I think you should stop the talking. For we don't belong together anyway. And I wanted to tell you from the start also that I have been engaged for an hour already to Klaus Dudy, who is just coming there."

And with that, she gave him a right hefty slap in the face with her heavy hand, and ran with her everlasting laughter back to the sunny village.

Ott Boll, however, just stood rigid for a while. Then he shook his massive steer's head, and stepped straightaway towards the approaching Klaus Dudy.

"You've gotten engaged to her then?" he inquired with threatening curtness.

"Yes," Klaus Dudy replied smugly, and he stretched his hands in his pockets in full proprietory superiority, and stood there with his legs apart. "That I have."

"So, you rogue," Ott continued with unnatural coldness. "Then, here, also take a little engagement gift from me."

Smack, he had struck, and swished so firmly and confidently in the middle of the other fellow's long face that the happy fiance stood seemingly blinded, and sun, moon, and stones sputter around him in circles.

"And now give her my regards many times over," the attacker added calmly, "and I'll come to your wedding."

"What?" the stricken man flailed as he leapt in the air in pain, "even to the wedding, you sordid weed? No, don't even dream of it. You're going in the hole, and for four weeks too, for look, I'm going straight now to report you. And you've been previously convicted too."

And so it happened. Ott Boll spent a secluded Pentecost in a lonely place, later signed up, and climbed ashore in Brazil just as the wedding organ was sounding for Klaus Dudy and Christin Dörthe, and Pastor Witt was making a wonderful sermon after the uplifting hymn "Whither thou goest, there will I go also."

Then three years went by.

But look, on a beautiful spring day, the sea whistled and flowed against the rocks, and the foam washed a happy music, who is striding there broadly and leisurely along the old balwark in a brand-new sailor's uniform and ribboned cap?

Look, it is Ott Boll. And he still has his hands flamboyantly in his pockets as if he had buried millions in them. On the old, now almost completely rotted away boat, the now much thinner Klaus Dudy sits, and now moves a little to the side as his old rival in love takes a seat next to him.

"Hi, Klaus."

"Hi, Ott."

"Well, how's it going?"

"What, how should it go?" Klaus Dudy cried venomously, and chewed on his fingernails. "If you hadn't been such a boor, and had to tell the girl all your infamous deeds, who knows if you wouldn't have then had her to my fortune."

"Look," the other grinned smugly, "that is so nice."

But the young husband became even more furious. "What," he shouted, "nice? Do you think perhaps one can live amicably with such an old viper, who has such accursedly strong bones? And you alone are to blame for the whole affair. But wait, this time I want to at least avenge myself. I still owe it to you." And with that, he rose, and struck with all his weight his homecoming friend directly on the nose. "And did you also know," he continued, "why I did this? Just so that you can now go and report me. For then I'll get, like you that time, my four weeks, and will be rid of her for that happy period."

"So?" Ott Boll said quite gently and evenly, while he wiped the bloody wound with his red handkerchief. "That's what you think, you Christian dolt! But for that you are much too stupid. Why will I provide for you such fine quarters which only serve for respectable people? No, I'll certainly report you, but you will have to pay me a large sum in compensation, for you are still without conviction. Except for Christin Dörthe. And that may well be enough. Thunderbolts, the Holy Ghost came over me strongly at the time. Well, and now give her my regards many times, and tell her if she wanted to mend one of my socks — she knows everything, then I'd come. And now, God bless you, and adieu!"

Shy Marik

A Tale from Bodden

Shy Marik

I heard the tale from old Kase Stöwesand, and Kase heard it from Marik Grapentin herself. Hence it is true, for Kase Stöwesand never spoke an untrue word, even if she sat crippled for thirty years by her low window and taught little children the "shivers" when she made faces at them with her yellow, wrinkled face. And the only thing which was a little incomprehensible with Kase was that she frequently quite unexpectedly would say to herself the words, "It is half past seven." That was, however, quite alright, for Kase had forty years ago lost her fiance to death at sea, and now she recalled frequently the time of his grave parting, and then she would murmur the hour just then to herself.

***

A heavy snowstorm was raging, and the storm was sweeping over the frozen bay so that the smooth path groaned under the noise. All around, you could discern nothing but grey twilight.

There I stood in Kase Stöwesand's little room, in which a little kerosene lamp was burning, and said, "I would like to get married now."

"Yes," she nodded, "then you must also get a Christmas tree, for a Christmas tree has a power."

"What do you mean, Kase?"

"Yes, and then she must not be shy either, otherwise it'll end up for you be like Jasper Grapentin, the helmsman, and his Marik. It was like this."

***

'Marik — Marik, come, look,' the helmsman Jasper Grapentin called as he entered the hall of his smug little house, and at the same time, he shook off the snow. 'Look, Marik, here I'm bringing you a fir. I chopped it down in the Dangerow woods, and even if you don't want to decorate it, today is Christmas Eve, such a thing is beautiful then. Now put out a few candles, I've brought wax with me too — here — and then we'll sit under it and think of something.'

With that the tall, fresh, powerful man, who was already in his thirties, planted the dark fir before his wife, who was much younger than him and as delicate and slender as a quite young girl. Which is actually what she was, since she had barely reached eighteen.

'Now quick, Marik.'

The young woman looked at him with her large, blue eyes for a moment astonished, but said neither yes nor no, instead nodded quickly, and began to busy herself by the tree. But this silent pandering was just awful for her. It was awful that she had married so soon, and that she possessed no will of her own, and above all, that she was so shy. From where did it come? Yes, she had been raised as an orphan by the harbour master, and she had been kept strictly, and scolded a lot, and in the end, she was delivered as half a child to the helmsman Jasper Grapentin, because he was a fresh fellow and displayed a joy in money, and had promised in addition to make her happy.

And that he also did in his way, quite cheerfully and right leniently, and he waited faithfully until everything was no longer so strange to her, her duties and the close togetherness and his pleasure in her. Only she thawed slowly — very, very slowly.

"Yes, yes, don't take a shy one," old Kase suggested.

***

But now it was flickering before the dark fir, it smelt of resin, and on the white tablecloth lay the presents which the couple had brought for each other. They only had to be practical objects — for the wife, material for a new dress; and for the husband, a pair of mittens — and there was no surprise bound up with them, because everything had been decided beforehand. But now they stood before the white table, and something like contentment passed through the small room.

'Quick, Marik,' Jasper said, 'now close the shutters over the windows. Then it will be even quieter. And then we will both be quite alone.'

Obediently she went, whereby she gauged with her large eyes a little from the side what he was probably aiming at with his words, and when the green wood now lay firmly against the panes, and only the snow which occasionally pecked at the panes interrupted the stillness, then Jasper said, rubbing his hands, 'Now come, mother' — it was the first time that he had called her that, 'now we want to sit here on the beautiful, new, black leather sofa, and tell each other something about the fir tree.'

With that he drew her next to himself, and the shy girl sat quite still by him with bated breath, for something was rising up towards her, something quiet, hidden, agreeable, which she could not explain.

'What do you want?' she whispered quite softly, and it seemed as if she were surprised that she had in fact spoken.

'Yes, mother,' he continued, and it was surely only by chance that he brushed her arm a little with his own. 'Now we are sitting here together, and it is properly quiet around us. But wait, it seems to me as if it could now soon get louder around us?'

At the same time, he let a sideglance fly over her again.

But hardly had he uttered the words than Marik started, turned deathly pale and later again seething red, and lifted her hands up against him as if she wanted to defend herself.

'My God,' she stammered.

'What is it?' Jasper laughed, and grasped heartily for her hand. 'Mother, what is to be ashamed of with that? It is just what dear God wants. The only thing that is bad about it, exists in that you —' But he interrupted himself, and tapped her on the back, and called out in the friskiest tone, 'Now, mother, we haven't spoken so much together in a long time. Truly, so much that my throat has become quite dry. How would it be if you now gave me something to drink? But you have surely just made your coffee again?'

'No,' she whispered quickly, 'I made grog for you.'

'Grog?' the helmsman repeated, completely taken aback at her attentiveness. 'Truly, mother, real grog? You thought of that? Oh, watch out, mother, it will still, it will still all be right — so much good hides in you.' At the same time, he sprung up, took the grog with the warm water to her, and then brought the glasses over with sugar and rum, and poured it in.

Jasper had to watch as she prepared everything, and when she raised her arm, then he also saw how fine and childlike it was! 'Mother,' he cried suddenly, after he had tasted the first glass, 'you are like a Christmas doll. And the courage — yes, yes, that will still come to you. Now drink!'

Then she really drank, and when, as a result, her blood was beginning to shimmer in her pale cheeks, and when the dark flames were flickering in her eyes, then wild thoughts passed through Jasper's soul until he suddenly had to grasp her hand to bring her fingers with a quick motion close to his ear.

'So, mother, you pinch there now, and you pluck at my beard too. You must now finally notice that you are actually the strongest here. Yes?'

He indeed felt her fingers on his skin, and even though she still pleaded 'oh Jasper', he did not let up.

'Now laugh too, my child,' he seemingly implored her. Then something amazing happened. She suddenly laughed bright and youthfully. And it was such an unaccustomed sound that the helmsman leapt up as if he wanted to investigate where the sound was coming from.

'You can?' came incredulously from his lips, 'you can?'

'Open up!' a voice meanwhile rang out from the snowstorm outside.

Torn from his dreams, Jasper opened the door. In the hall stood the postman who shoved a letter towards him. 'From Wismar,' he boomed. Then the bell on the front door tinkled again, and the intruder had disappeared again.

Silence reigned again. The helmsman sat at the table, and read. The tree's candles were almost burnt down, and Jasper was so engrossed that he hardly noticed how attentively and tensely this young child who was his wife followed his actions.

Finally a question was released by her lips, short and clenched, 'Jasper, will you accept — will you accept the proposal?'

He lifted his head, his eyes were shining their own steely brilliance which they constantly showed when the talk was about money.

'Marik,' he responded in a low voice, 'two hundred talers a month — and at the end, a thousand marks bestowed. That will never be offered to me again.'

'And how long will you be away?'

'Oh,' he said offhand — 'just two years. And up there in the ice regions, I can save everything. Oh, watch out, mother, I'll come back a rich man. And then I'll pay for my own little steamship, and then you'll be a captain's wife. — You aren't saying anything at all?'

But she remained silent. And it was again the awful thing that this loudly pounding heart could not speak.

She sat in a corner, and while he bent down over the writing anew, she gazed into the dying candles, and listened to the hammering in her breast, and heard how the ice cracked on the bay, sharp and bursting like a cry of pain.

***

After four years, Jasper Grapentin returned home. His ship had been iced-in up there so that nothing had been heard of him.

It was an older man who knocked one morning on the door, a little stooped, with furrows on his forehead, and with a long full beard which exhibited a silvery edge at its tips. In his hand, the man was carrying a tiny little fir tree.

'Good morning,' the arrival said, and hesitated as a sturdy, limber woman stood before him with a girl of perhaps three years, 'Are you Marik?'

She answered, while examining him strangely, with a loud, clear voice, 'So I am called, but what do you want here? — I don't need a Christmas tree.'

'Yes, Marik,' the arrival replied in a soft voice. 'Today is again Christmas Eve, and I cut the tree in the Dangerow woods. But you have become sturdy and beautiful,' he added slowly, and his voice, which he had seldom used in the eternal ice, sounded timid and emotional, 'and now lay your arms around my neck, for see, I am Jasper.'

Then the woman took a step back, and pulled her child with her so that it screamed. Then she spoke dismissively, 'If you are Jasper, then I am pleased that you remain alive. And this here is your child. But I don't want to put my arms around your neck, for I can barely find myself in you, you look so different. I'm not used to such tenderness. But while you were away, I kept everything as it was, and the work has done me good. Now sit down, and drink a swallow of something warm.'

The man sat down, and shook his head. Then he pulled out his wallet, and counted several thousand marks onto the table. But the woman walking back and forth busily did not give them a glance. So it remained the entire day. She did not waste any words. Only when the helmsman once wanted timidly to stroke the blond head of the little girl, he had to shake his head again bashfully, and drew his fingers back as though ashamed. In the afternoon, he went away. When he returned home in the evening, the little fir tree he had chopped in the Dangerow woods was burning there, and next to it in the alcove, the little girl was sleeping, for it was already late.

But the silence did not end. They both sat quietly on the black leather sofa, and looked at the tree. But how they had both transformed through the years: she, upright, blossomed, confident — and he, weary, exhausted, and depressed; a man who had become shy and timid in the eternal stillness of the world of ice; only holding the wallet in his hand like an exoneration.

They sat thus for a long, long time.

But when he had to think of how he had left there at the time, unloving, just in the moment when the shy soul next to him wanted to open up, then it cut him through the chest, and his forehead bent forward heavily until it rested on the red beech table, something like a sob shook through his tough body when he did not otherwise stir.

And again a long period of time passed. The fir tree gave off its scent, and the candles flickered in the draught, and so the rapt man did not notice how a hand touched his ear quite gently, and then plucked his beard too, and how at the same time, around the lips of his sturdy wife, a quite peculiar, overwhelmed, and yet victorious smile was playing. — —

***

"Yes, yes, the shy ones," old Kase suggested, "they have so much that can not be unravelled — that you can believe."

Uncle Pökel

Or the Treasure Seeking at Knüppelhagen

Uncle Pökel

I would never have believed that I would be telling this piece of my youth once more at length, and my neighbour, the merchant Albrecht is proved correct, when he says, "He's a good old fellow, but he can't seem to keep his mouth shut." With that he takes aim at me. — Unfortunately, it is a bad piece, for I promised the main character in my telling, my dear old uncle Pökel, firmly and confidently many years ago that I wanted to keep absolutely quiet about this incident. And when he had calmed down about it, he had shaken my hand, and proposed thus quite reflective and self-assured, "Well, Jörg, then you can bank on me, for I'll come to Berlin sometime, and dig for you such a little private treasure out of the ground. For I'm a success at it. And if that at Knüppelhagen was not a success for me, then that lies on the old blockheads who interrupted me in my under-standing; and Jörg" — here my uncle Pökel stuck his hands in his pockets quite smugly, and stood before me as if he were the owner of Ali Baba's cave with all its treasures, or as if Bleichröder or Rothschild had just begged him imploringly to become their partner — "and Jörg," he said, "in Berlin, there still lies treasures from the old Greeks and Romans, — who were once resident there, and if I just climb between them once, then it'd have to go to the devil if I couldn't find the piles of money. And then you know me, my boy."

Oh yes, I knew you well enough, you old faithful soul, and how I always rejoiced when the muttering began in the little town, "Uncle Pökel is here again! — Have you heard? —No, what? — He wants to look for treasure here again! — What, all that again? — Well, it would lie in Father Krüger's manure heap. — Thunderbolts! Krüger's cow makes gold?"

So it went when you entered the small town, dear old Uncle Pökel, with your gaunt, thin figure and the long, long legs which you always had stuck into yellow Nanking trousers, and with your old venerable face which constantly looked as solemn as that of a prophet from the Old Testament wanting to prophesise something to his old Jews. And when you really had fetched from the the farmer Schröder's rape fields a little pot with six five groschen pieces in it, then your fellow citizens almost wanted to give you a torchlight procession, and that evening a scientific association was founded for the pot, of which they made you President, — and then a beautiful punch was brewed in the little pot, and my own father got into a very bad mood from this beautiful drink at this beautiful celebration.

Dear God, how long ago it is now already. The torches are extinguished, and the torches of life are also extinguished, and my father has already been sleeping a long time, and even my dear Uncle Pökel has climbed down deep, deep into the earth and is lying there quite still — and has himself been taken as a great treasure into the earth — a great treasure of love and human cheerfulness, and a warm, soft heart, a human heart — and this treasure which nobody will detect anymore, it must remain lying under the cold earth, and only on the Day of Judgment will the great, the divine treasure seeker take him up into the heights, and take a look at his heart, and say, "That is genuine, that is pure gold, and that goes into my best treasure chamber." —

Uncle Pökel, until then, however, a good length of time must pass, and when I recently in my old home town wandered over to your grave, no stone effigy lay on it. Only a couple of birds sang on your grave, and a few yellow buttercups blossomed in the place, looking almost like your yellow Nanking trousers. And then it occurred to me — how would it be if I attempted to lay a monument to you myself. See, and then it was almost to me as if you had raised your old head up out of the ground and laughed, "Boy, you don't want perhaps to bring a stonemason to my grave?" No, Uncle Pökel, this will be a written monument — also have no fear that it will become too discriminating, for look, it can only be a little modest monument, because I am myself only a little modest stonemason "with the pen". And now sleep well, Uncle Pökel; I am beginning and telling it thus.

Chapter One

It was in the twilight hour. The snowflakes were falling softly from the grey sky down onto the firmly frozen earth. Everything was still, as if there were something to listen to here. The old poplars stood stiff and rigid with their white shirts before the lonely forsaken farmhouse of Knüppelhagen, and the old poplars looked as if they also wanted to go to their white bed, but still had to check first whether the sun also, which still stood in the sky like a little, rosy-cheeked girl who did not want to go to sleep yet, whether the sun was also going nicely and well-behaved to her white bed. — The sun went into its white bed, a little hesitantly, as if it still wanted to stay up a little longer — and just as it threw back its last glance, a deep, aching sigh could be heard below on the earth.

It was not the poplars; who was it?

It was a tall, slender girl with plain golden hair and a pair of dark blue eyes, and the dark blue eyes looked out from a pale, lovely face as wistfully after the sun as if hope had just taken leave of her and would not be returning anymore at all.

"Lena, was that you?" a sharp voice asked behind her, and a tall, strong woman, who had been sitting until then in the warm room by the bed of her husband, Krischan Sellentin, looked to her.

"No, mother, nothing's the matter," Lena replied from out the window.

"Well, I thought so, my daughter, and now bring your father his tea."

Lena stood up, brought her father his tea, and at the same time, brushed her white hand over his hair, "Father, is it getting better?"

From the bed, something belched with a hideous, hoarse sound, as if an old bass trumpet were being tried for the first time, "No, Lena — my neck, it's still ever so stiff — and my lower back — my accursed lower back — as stiff as a wagon shaft — now I've been looking constantly at the ceiling for all of two days — and there is nothing at all to see but a pair of dopey flies sleeping there."

"Krischan," his wife admonished, "you must have patience."

"Who has patience," he tooted again from the bed — "when a man has nothing to see but flies — do — do —; the devil would fool them."

"Father," Lena objected gently, "the doctor told me today" — —

"Eh what, the doctor — such an indecent fellow — he wants to convince me that my illness is named like a hussy — Flo Enza, the old creature is called."

"Hussy?" Mrs Sellentin called out sharply here, and immediately straightened up. — "Krischan, here — in front of Lena? Be completely silent!"

"What? — more being silent? And I don't even know any Flo Enza?" he wailed from the bed again.

Lena had turned quite red; now she said, "Father, you haven't understood the doctor properly, he meant you had influenza."

"It's all the same to me, Lena. — Influenza, ugh, that's a horse sickness. — Am I a horse? — Lena, look — —" here he wanted to provide still further explanations that he was not a horse, but he fell back in his bed, and again began groaning terribly, "Yes — yes —, yes — now I have it again —, I must not stir — I can't be rid of the damned flies — it's in my neck again — mother, read to me from the book — that is still the best."

"Well, Sellentin, then lie properly still though. This is a very religious book, they tell me it's from Strelitz, for I want to have something edifying for you."

"Well, what's it called then?"

Mrs Sellentin wet her finger, and opened the first page, "The book is called — Olympus, or — My–to–lo–gy of the Greeks and Romans with inclusion of the Egyptian, Nordic and Indian Divine Teachings, by A. H. Petiskus."

Such a tiny lost sigh came from the bed, "Mother, this will surely be very pious?"

And now his dear wife began to read about all the old stuff with gods, and Krischan looked up ever piously as if he were sending a thousand prayers up to Zeus and Apollo, but in truth, he was constantly watching both his flies; and Lena also sat at the window again, and stared out into the night.

Outside, the snowflakes were still falling, and the tall beautiful girl looked as raptly into the driving snow as if someone whom she was fond of over all else were striding out there. But that one of whom she was thinking could not come. He had just that day written in a letter that his father, the rich estate owner Dankward, wanted to disown him if he associated himself any longer with the poor farmgirl; and she herself should now decide. — And she had decided straightaway. She had returned all his presents, and she had torn his letters into little scraps. — That hurt, poor Lena, it hurt a lot. — And when she now stared out into the snow flurry, a strange thought came to her.

The earth had broken faith with the heavens, and the heavens were also tearing up the letters from their old beloved, and the snowflakes which were now falling, they were the scraps of the letters, and they were falling straight into the disloyal earth's face. — — Then the dog jumped up, the door opened — and in stepped — —

"Yes, thunderbolts! That is surely Pökel?" Krischan cried out from his bed, and again made a sad attempt to get away from his flies.

Now his wife stood up; Lena sprang up as well to receive Uncle Pökel's summer overcoat. For he wore a summer overcoat in winter; he made a virtue of hardship, and said it was for the "ventilation". — And when they had now unwrapped him, Uncle Pökel said with his old solemn voice, "What's this here? Krischan lying in bed and with a red handkerchief bound about his head."

— — Here he stepped up to the bed. "Krischan, good evening, why aren't you looking at me — what's wrong with you then?"

Krischan also wanted to turn to his old friend, only he could not.

"Oh yes — yes — yes," he wailed, "Pökel, Pökel, I have something with a hussy."

Uncle Pökel looked around quite gravely, then he seized the patient's hand, and said, "Don't upset yourself. — You have it surely a bit in the head?"

"Yes, Pökel," he groaned again, "the two flies — I will probably soon now be a fly myself."

"So, so, Krischan, 'a fly'," Uncle Pökel nodded, and turned quite pale, and he whispered softly to the woman, "My poor friend, how long has he been all so bonkers?"

"What, would he not be in his right mind?" the woman now cried out, and her patience was breaking now! "He has the flu because he was running around last week with bare feet in the snow because of his chilblains." —

"What? Just chilblains?" Uncle Pökel asked, very relieved, took a chair, and relaxed again at once, "then show me your feet please, Krischan. I have some understanding of that. — You must take your big toe in the mouth, and say seven Our Fathers, then it'll be okay."

Here he fell silent, for Mrs Sellentin had taken the book, and hit him with it on the knee, "Pökel, Pökel — will you please stop with your magic? I don't want that in my house! You will ruin me yet." —

She wanted to preach a bit more still, but Uncle Pökel stopped her effort by raising both hands in the air, almost over his head, as if he wanted to tear out all Madame Sellentin's hair, or let off a terribly direful curse from the Old Testament.

"Madame Sellentin," he said solemnly, and now he also looked up at Krischan's flies, "I tell you, today is the day and the hour and the sign of a happy success — for the planets are aligned, and the moons are aligned, and the satellites are aligned — — — —"

"But your five sense aren't aligned," Mrs Sellentin shouted, and threw the book so that all Olympus shook.

"You should keep your moons at a distance. Have you understood me now?"

"Mrs Stellentin, I just mean the constellations — because of which, I came here."

Mrs Stellentin threw herself onto her chair, and struggled for air, "Eh what, Pökel, don't lie, you came because you thought that we had slaughtered all our pigs. — Well, I would have liked to have had you to dinner with us too, but I had to postpone because of Krischan's illness. — For today there is easily digestible food for the ill, and Lena should see to that right away."

With these words, Lena stood up, and went into the kitchen.

Pökel wanted now to apologise, and blathered on a lot about Mars and Venus, which were a pair of excellent planets for treasure seeking, and that Mrs Sellentin was pushing away her fortune with her feet because she had not once let him dig under the great oak in her garden; but when he wanted to also explain about the planet Jupiter, Krischan's bed began at once to move, like the white mountain Hekla when it starts spitting fire, and when Pökel said Jupiter once more, a proper earthquake broke forth in the mountain, only that instead of thunder, such a screeching laughter was heard, "Ju–pi–Ju–pi–ter–, yes —, yes —, Ju–pi — — —"

"God preserve me," Uncle Pökel blessed himself. "Krischan, what do you want with the old heathen god?"

Only now the stream of lava was almost shooting out of Hekla's bed, the mountain began dancing so.

"Pökel — tell me," — thus it rolled out of the pillows — "Jupiter, that's the old smutty one surely?"

"What do you mean, smutty one?" Uncle Pökel echoed, affronted as it were.

"Well, mother, you know, the old fellow from the book who is always after the little human girls."

Mrs Sellentin sank into her chair, and slapped her hands together. "Krischan," she burst out, struck to the core, "and that is for your edification? No, I've unhinged my eyes from my head before Pökel; ugh, shame on you, shame on you, shame on you."

After she had said this for the third time, she too vanished into the kitchen, and Krischan lay down, and wanted to have some information from both his flies over what was actually happening around him here. After a while, he began again, "Pökel!"

"Well, what is it then again?"

"That's an infernal fellow."

"Who? Me?"

"No, old Jupiter."

"The devil, let him be."

"No, the way that old man started it?"

"God preserve me, what's all this again?"

"Well, that he could marry his real sister."

"So?" Pökel asked, displeased with it, "he did that?"

"And even had children with her," Krischan tried to add, sitting up, but erupted over the misdeeds of Zeus in a piteous lament, "Yes, yes, my neck — that the great prince of the Greeks also admitted to such a thing though — ow! my back — that would be almost like if I wanted to court my own Lena."

"Lie down again," Pökel said. "Apropos, Lena — what is with the little girl, she looks fairly unsettled to me."

"Oh, Pökel, she agitates me over her circumstances."

"Over what?" Pökel asked, as if he could not trust his ears.

"Oh, over my awful circumstances and over the old estate owner Dankward, who plays himself up as a rich man."

And now Uncle Pökel learnt the entire sad story.

"Thunderbolts," he said at the end, "that's no fun — my little Lena — and at the same time, my planets were lined up so prettily. — Well, wait a minute, Krischan."

With that, he too went into the kitchen, and Krischan lay again under his Hekla, and could make two observations. — Firstly, that there was much crying and kissing in the kitchen.

"Thunderbolts, why has Pökel smothered my family with kisses?"

And secondly, that in the in-between time, one of the two flies had crept a stretch towards the other. "Is it not possible, they will now surely begin soon to play the merry-go-round," Krischan wondered to himself, and lost himself in deep thought.

At supper, only a little was eaten. The table stood before Krischan's bed, but the host could not stir, Mrs Stellentin was annoyed over Petiskus and old Dankward, Lena only over the young Dankward, and Uncle Pökel was always throwing a sorrowful look at pale Lena, and a pleased one at his piece of sausage, but slowly he sank as well into deep thought until he finally slammed his fist on the table, crying out, "Fine — now I have it."

"What, Uncle Pökel?" asked Lena, who had been quite startled.

"Oh, nothing, I have merely planned something very serious."

Mrs Sellentin heard that, and it coincided entirely with her annoyance over Petiskus, "Pökel," she scolded gently, "you will not want me to participate again with your superstitious rubbish?"

"No," Pökel said, certain of victory, "my dear friend, planets and satellites, they are astronomical constellations and not superstition. — In addition, I am not superstitious, and when I hear such things, I admonish the people to see reason, e.g. your neighbour over there,

Mrs Muchown. — What nonsense the old woman propounded to me the other week! — The woman suffered a murder in the night or, as they say in High German, she had a nightmare; and now just think what the old woman believes now. 'Mr Pökel,' she says to me, 'there are men who have eyebrows that are grown together over the nose, and these men, they must walk around at night, and go into strange rooms, and seize other people who are lying there sleeping, and squeeze them, and that is the incubus. — And if you say to such a spirit, "I invite you to lunch tomorrow", then the spirit must break off' — Mrs Stellentin, have you ever heard such perversion?"

It was possible that Mrs Sellentin had not yet heard such a thing, but at the moment, she bent forward, and looked quite anxiously at Uncle Pökel's nose.

"What?" the guest asked, and took up his napkin, "have I smeared sausage over myself?"

"No, Pökel — God forbid! But your eyebrows are also grown together," Mrs Sellentin cried, and moved her chair back a little. "You are quite well?"

When Uncle Pökel saw her fearful face, he became very annoyed, he stood up, took his candle, and said, "Don't be offended, Mrs Sellentin, but what did you want to say by that? Did I ever squeeze you in the night? — Or have I ever squeezed Krischan? — Krischan," he flared up, "tell me, have I squeezed you in the night?"

"No," rang out from the bed, "you haven't engaged yourself in such a thing yet, Pökel."

"And have I perhaps squeezed Lena?"

"Pökel," the woman relented, "I did not mean it like that —"

"Did not mean it so — so? — but you wanted to make me into a spirit! — do I look like a spirit that has to vanish at the first rooster's crow? — Have I ever vanished from your place at the first rooster's crow?"

"Pökel, I'm convinced that you aren't a spirit, now settle down, old friend."

"Not a spirit? — wonderful — but I don't do vanishing either — with your permission, I'll sleep in your loft; and now — good night, Krischan, and get well."

With that he went, and Lena lit the way above for him. But when they were both climbing up the small steps, Uncle Pökel suddenly stopped, and said he had to go down once more, and when Lena wanted in astonishment to ask him what he still had to seek in the snow, Uncle Pökel embraced the tall beautiful girl, gave her a tender kiss on her red mouth, and whispered, "Lena — my sweet Lena — don't cry Lena — everything will come right again. — Uncle Pökel is still here. — And the planets and moons are aligned — I'll help you, my little girl."

And with that, he went down the stairs again, and vanished into the winter's night.

Chapter Two

Now, my most gracious reader, you must excuse me; I don't know anymore in fact how my tale continues. But I know better what you will say to this opening.

"What?" you will reproach me, "first you lead us around by the nose so that we all must listen to your rubbish, how Uncle Pökel wears a summer overcoat, and Krischan has something to do with Flo Enza, and how Mrs Sellentin furthers her acquaintance with Olympus, and that there are people with eyebrows grown together; we have had to endure such utter rubbish with you, and now finally, when you have something proper to tell or, as they say, when the moment of suspense has arrived —, then you want to leave us sitting in the lurch and make yourself scarce?"

My most gracious reader, I have something very learned to answer to that.

Old Plato, — that is, however, not the old instrument maker who, in our newspapers, constantly touts his harmoniums and barrel-organs to us — no, the old philosoper Plato, who had a hellishly witty head, who once said the life of a man was "so–so". We don't know at all whether we see now in fact what happens outside, or whether we do not see it. It could all possibly signify only the appearance or shadow of reality. Like when a man were sitting his whole life long in a dark cave with his back to the light, and looks constantly at a stone wall. And on this wall constantly scurry the shadows of all that which happens outside in reality, and the man would then say that just these shadows were the truth. — You see, my most gracious reader, it was always so for me with Uncle Pökel when I ever wanted to ask him about this night and what he actually carried out then. He had then likewise constantly turned his back to me, and looked at the wall, and mumbled all sorts of words to himself, and waved about with his hands as if he were grappling with utterly revolting shadows, and I was meant to have made some sense from that.

Now, I will not let you sit in ignorance, and would prefer at any risk to narrate further, but if we now come anyway to a dark place, then you must just have the feeling as though we are all now sitting with each other in the dark cave, and Plato and Uncle Pökel's strange shadows are appearing and disappearing before us. — —

When the hour struck half past eleven, Uncle Pökel came with two almost frozen, little boys creeping into the yard, and looked around a little uncertainly.

Where he had gotten the boys from, that I do not know, does not concern me at all either, they are already two of the dim shadows, but I believe that they were the two half-grown boys of the old councillor Pagel, whom their father had apprenticed to Uncle Pökel for his treasure seeking.

The moon hid behind dark clouds, the snow glittered on the frozen earth, and it was bitterly cold. "Boys," Uncle Pökel whispered to his apprentices, "didn't you see a black shadow before us, which drifted through the garden, and vanished into the air?"

But the boys were still too dimwitted at treasure seeking, and said they saw nothing.

"Well, then good," their teacher suggested to them, "and now keep your mouths shut. With treasure seeking, not a single word may be spoken, otherwise it's all over. Look, there is the oak, and now we'll wait until the clock strikes twelve."

And then the three stood there, and waited for the witching hour.

Thus sometimes a man stands, and waits for a specific hour when fortune shall come, and at the same time, fortune already stands behind him, and she is a white, rosy-cheeked, wondrous girl who waits with heart pounding for the man to embrace her; and the man does not do it, and thinks fortune must first come to him; and then he suddenly hears such a gentle rustling, and when he looks around, then the rosy-cheeked girl of fortune is going from him in tears, and behind him stands Mrs Sorrow with her grey cloak and grins at him, and says, "Blockhead, now you can wait a long time for the little girl, but I, my boy, will keep you company for a bit here."

Uncle Pökel also heard such a gentle rustling above in the bare oak, but when he stretched his long nose up, he noticed nothing, and now he stood again, and looked at Lena's window. There a pair of icicles were hanging down; they almost looked as if they were tears. And his apprentices, the little Pagels, stood by him, and the tears were also running over their cheeks, only that was from the cold, and because they were still so inexperienced in these affairs of magic.

Then the hour struck twelve from the village. — The dull blows rolled through the night, and at the same time, the wind began to blow, and the oak creaked and groaned as if spirits lived in its branches and were stretching their white hands out to Uncle Pökel.

"Now at it," the latter whispered, as if he were in a mood for engaging now in a battle with spirits, "now dig it up, boys."

At this command, the digging began. In deep silence, the earth was hacked into, and Pökel's apprentices attacked the matter straightaway so heartily that if Schliemann had been watching, he would have immediately engaged them for excavating Troy. Thus the hole became deeper and deeper, and the wind howled ever more eerily, and the oak groaned and whimpered as if it were a miser whose treasure they were wanting to take. — And I believe, they would have lifted the treasure too if it had in fact been there, and if one of the apprentices had not broken off so daftly.

"Mr Pökel," a loud voice suddenly cried.

"Boy — God protect you — will you shut your mouth!"

"Yes, Mr Pökel," he crowed back, "but look, up there — the black thing with the fiery eyes — it's the devil crawling to us to break our necks. — I will protect myself!" — And with that, both apprentices threw away their mattocks, and ran like the wind out of the garden. From a distance, they could still be heard, "The devil — the devil is walking in Sellentin's garden!"

Something crept down from the oak, sat on a branch, and flashed fiery eyes at Uncle Pökel. The spirit had clasped its tail between its feet.

"Eh, eh," my dear Uncle Pökel now stuttered, and was almost shaking at the knees, "what is that?"

He straightened up, cleared his throat, and said in a quite soft voice, "Who are you?" — No answer. — The devil sat there, and continued to act as if it wanted to immediately fall on the treasure seeker's neck.

"Don't you hear? — Who are you? — and why have you come here? — I can't believe though that you are the devil? I am Pökel, do you want something from me?" —

Only the devil was not in favour of the modern ideas, it brought its tail forward, and began to strike Pökel with it. The tail was pointed like a nail.

"God bless me," Pökel stammered pitiably, "such a thing, we never wagered on," and now he executed a leap, and shot more dead than alive into the kitchen of Mrs Sellentin to search for a light there. But he did not find one, just threw a couple of plates on the ground, tore though in his eagerness to the bedroom where the married couple were slumbering, and now stood, fighting for air, in the doorway. They had lit a night light in the room because of Krischan's illness, and Krischan, who had been dreaming constantly of Pökel's grown-together eyebrows, sat up in fright, looked at his old friend, and began to wail dreadfully, "Mother — there he is — there stands Pökel — and now he wants to come squeeze us."

Mrs Sellentin woke up, saw Pökel in her sanctum, and — whoosh! — she crept under her covers until nothing more was to be seen of her.

Uncle Pökel, however, was also robbed of speech by fear, he could only raise his arms up, but this strengthened Krischan even more in his opinion, "Pökel — I invite you to lunch tomorrow," he wailed with his stiff neck. "There will also be pea soup with pigs' ears, but I beg you, old friend, don't hop on my chest."

And when he had said that, he too vanished from the upper world, merely rumbled from under the covers like a bit before, "For lunch — for lunch — ow, my neck!"

I do not know now whether Uncle Pökel had given a little taste of the incubus's squeeze, but I don't think so, for he found himself already a few seconds later as a complete fellow again before his oak tree, and this time, he carried a candle in his hand as if he wanted to hold a procession before the devil. But where was the devil? It was sitting in the hole in the earth, and began at once to implore, "Mr Pökel — oh, I beg you — help me out of this damned hole — I have dislocated my entire foot."

"So, so," Uncle Pökel said, "what has happened? My devil begins to talk hellishly polite." And now he illuminated its face.

"What? Fritz Dankward, you're the devil?" Uncle Pökel cried now, stunned, and held the candle under his nose. "Sir, — I don't know at all — what the devil cajoled you up our oak tree?"

"Mr Pökel, later — first just help me out of this hole."

"Eh, no, stay sitting there for a bit. It is a good cooling off for that letter you wrote to our Lena. Well? First such a letter, and then this climbing in our oak tree? — Sir, I believe it must look enviable in your head."

Now the devil turned wild. "Sir, what does that concern you?"

"What does it concern me? It concerns me a lot. — When such a slicker comes, and first turns the head of such a little inexperienced girl, and then wants nothing more with her, and plays the devil out here. — Well, I will summon the people here at once so that they can look at the spirit up close."

Then he acted as if he were walking away.

"For God's sake, Mr Pökel, stay here, I want to explain everything to you, I — I was merely climbing the tree because — —"

"Well, because?"

"Because" — And now he began to talk quite meekly from out of the hole, "Uncle Pökel, if you are currently a widower, you must have once had a bride." —

"Yes," Uncle Pökel said, "she was a sweet girl."

"Now see, Uncle Pökel, I could not have endured it, because I fancied Lena, but" — here he sighed deeply — "but my father, who can't be moved on this, he wants to chase me out of house and home, and then I was deceived, and wrote the miserable letter."

"Yes, that is all very nice, but what were you looking for up the tree then?"

"Uncle Pökel, understand, I merely wanted to see my dear once more! —"

"What, me?"

"Oh, Lena — she's lying over there now in her room, and I am so close to her, and don't know how to help myself."

Uncle Pökel looked at him a while gravely, then he said, "Now listen to me. Firstly, Lena is much too good for you, — do you understand me?"

"Mr Pökel — —"

"Secondly, you are a despicable fellow of a fiance."

"Mr Pökel — —"

"And thirdly — in your father's head, the devil surely plays the kettle drum?"

"Mr Pökel, I don't understand you at all."

"That I believe, but I want to interpret that for you. — Well? Such a fellow as you, who always clings to his father's coattails?"

"Mr Pökel, should I let the beautiful estate go?"

"No, sir, then let Lena go," Pökel cried in blazing fury.

"Oh, I can't do that either."

"Now look what an irritating guest you are?" Uncle Pökel scolded. — "Young man, I feel pity for you. Has it never occurred to you that the many estate owners in the vicinity here would like to employ a superintendent? Is that not an adequate position?"

All of a sudden, young Dankward sprang from the hole, "Uncle Pökel, are you serious?"

"Well, do you think, sir, that I want to have fun here with my cold feet?"

"God — Mr Pökel, it occurred to me often already, but now I am firmly decided."

"Young man," Uncle Pökel said, "then you have decided on something very sensible, and if you'll take my advice further, then contact me. And now good night, my entire body is shivering."

"Uncle Pökel — just one more word; — may I just speak to Lena for a few minutes alone?"

"That's not bad," Pökel grinned. "Such a subtle fellow — sir, since you played the devil, you have taken on such demonic views. — But now is enough. Now you will march right out of the garden. — One, two — three!"

With that they parted.

When Uncle Pökel strode to his room, whereby he also had to pass that of Lena, the door was a little open, and through the crack, a lovely, blond girl's countenance was looking, and at this opportunity, Uncle Pökel set eyes on a white arm, at the sight of which Fritz Dankward would certainly have lost his mind.

"Uncle Pökel," a shaking voice whispered, "who was that man down below? And what sort of voice was that?"

But now I am ashamed almost for my lead character. What did our Uncle Pökel do? He seized the head and the white arm, and kissed them in turns again and again and, at the same time, he whispered, "Be still, Lena, be completely still. That was God's voice. And now fortune will return, and love also; and what have I always said? — The planets and the moons are aligned."

The moon gleamed its silver a little later into the two rooms. In the first, Lena lay on her knees, folded her hands, and looked earnestly up at the beaming disc. And the moon glimmered, and blazed its answer, "Now fortune is coming, Lena, now fortune is coming."

In the other room, Uncle Pökel sat in his bed, and pondered, "That with the planets tallied, but that with the little Pagels did not tally, and no man can credit that to me to my disadvantage."

With this thought, he fell asleep. Only his friend, the moon, laughed down at him, and asked a little mockingly, "Pökel, haven't you found a treasure? I heard something like that."

"No, old friend," Pökel replied crossly, "I believe not."

"But you have found it," the moon contradicted.

"You lie!" Pökel cried.

"Man, take care of your words," the moon grinned. "Didn't you find Lena's treasure? And doesn't a man count for more than silver and gold? And look, because you are such an old honest fellow, I will do something for you too."

And all of a sudden, it seemed as if small brooks and fountains of real silver were flowing down from the moon, straight to Uncle Pökel's bed. And in the brooks, pretty, golden fish with louis d'ors on their bodies were playing. And Uncle Pökel saw himself in his dream as he sat there with a silver crown on his head, but with bare legs, and how he fished up with a net one after the other of the golden fish, until the moon finally said, "Now you are rich enough, Pökel, now adieu."

And now we let Uncle Pökel sleep in his wealth, and say quite softly so that he does not awake, the same thing that the moon wished, that is, "adieu". And that I do herewith.

About the Publisher

Our mission is to provide translations into English of the complete works of neglected major European writers. We do not cherry-pick works that seem the most marketable, but rather seek to provide a complete collection of each writer's works so that readers can follow the writer's development and decide on its merits for themselves.

http://www.facebook.com/KANitzPublishing